Christmas 2015
in Berlin

Berlin Tales

Fröhliche Weihnacht und ein gesundes neues Jahr!

Berlin Tales

Stories translated by

Lyn Marven

Edited by

Helen Constantine

OXFORD

UNIVERSITY PRESS

OXFORD

UNIVERSITY PRESS

Great Clarendon Street, Oxford OX2 6DP

Oxford University Press is a department of the University of Oxford.
It furthers the University's objective of excellence in research, scholarship,
and education by publishing worldwide in

Oxford New York

Auckland Cape Town Dar es Salaam Hong Kong Karachi
Kuala Lumpur Madrid Melbourne Mexico City Nairobi
New Delhi Shanghai Taipei Toronto

With offices in

Argentina Austria Brazil Chile Czech Republic France Greece
Guatemala Hungary Italy Japan Poland Portugal Singapore
South Korea Switzerland Thailand Turkey Ukraine Vietnam

Oxford is a registered trade mark of Oxford University Press
in the UK and in certain other countries

Published in the United States
by Oxford University Press Inc., New York

General introduction © Helen Constantine 2009
Introduction, selection, notes, and translation © Lyn Marven 2009

The moral rights of the authors have been asserted
Database right Oxford University Press (maker)

First published 2009

British Library Cataloguing in Publication Data

Data available

Library of Congress Cataloging in Publication Data

Library of Congress Control Number: 2009924591

Typeset by SPI Publisher Services, Pondicherry, India
Printed in Great Britain
on acid-free paper by
Clays Ltd., St. Ives plc

ISBN 978–0–19–955938–1

8

Contents

Picture Credits

General Introduction

This volume is one of a series, each being a collection of stories about capital cities. The city is always the starting point for the particular story; but often the physical location assumes a wider significance as the story is told. Through the eyes of the writer who has formed an individual relationship with a certain place, readers may come to see aspects of it that have so far remained hidden to them. In this book of tales chosen and translated by Lyn Marven, we shall, like many tourists, visit the sights in Berlin, but we shall also discover other worlds where past and present intermingle and where the city comes alive differently in the imaginations of both writer and reader.

Readers of this book will know that Berlin, the third most-visited European capital after Paris and London, has had what is perhaps the most dramatic and difficult history of all European cities. In the 1920s, during the Weimar Republic, it was the violently energetic metropolis, the cultural capital of Europe, site of a great florescence in all the arts. Hitler put a stop to that when he and his Nazis came to power in 1933. Artists, scientists, liberal thinkers left in their thousands and emigrated. Berlin became the capital of persecution and war. One surreal and sad little story here, by Günter Kunert, concerns a man called David Platzker who rolls up his street like a carpet and escapes before the deportations, only to find when he returns that the carpet no longer fits the old street where he used to live. By the beginning of 1943 most of Berlin's Jewish community had been deported and murdered in the camps, and by the end of the Second World War much of the city had been destroyed by Allied bombs and Soviet artillery. What remained was divided into four sectors, overseen by the Soviet, American, English, and French governments, but deteriorating relations between East and West during the Cold War resulted, in 1961, in the sudden building of the Wall that severed the streets, divided families and kept the citizens of the East from moving West. The Wall, a powerful symbol of post-war division, was breached and began to be demolished in 1989. This history is the background but also the *raison d'être* of many of these stories from a turbulent and beleaguered city.

In April 1999, one city again, Berlin became the capital of the unified Federal Republic. Its twenty-three districts have undergone—and are still undergoing—one of the most radical reconstructions in Europe. Today it is an energetic, lively, forward-looking city, in the very spirit of the twenty-first century. Today's Berlin is young and liberal, relatively cheap, easy to live in, with an enviable transport system, arts venues, orchestras, and museums. This renewal is palpable in the stories by, for example, Carmen Francesca Banciu or Ulrike Draesner. But Berlin is also a city which cannot forget its past—walk around it and there will be reminders, deliberate or involuntary, wherever you go, from the Reichstag to Potsdamer Platz, from Kreuzberg to the Jewish museum. Many of the writers here are attempting to make sense of the enormous changes that have taken place in their lifetime. Monika Maron treats the strange experience of coming back to Berlin, her birthplace, and trying to reconnect with her past self in scenes from her childhood which 'appear and dissolve again'. She comes to realize that the two halves of the city are part of a whole, 'that their parts belonged to the same body'.

Like all cities, but perhaps more than most, Berlin is a place of remembering and forgetting. A young journalist who traced the path of the Wall with some difficulty in May 2007 found that parts had been almost eradicated by new building, but that a cobbled path, a *Mauerweg*, had begun to be built along the line of it as a guide to the twenty-first-century tourist. Older Berliners, who lived through the division, may prefer to forget this marker of the history of Berlin, but younger people often take a certain pride in it as they do in the museums, plaques, and monuments. The remarkable new buildings are a way for many to forget and remember at the same time. This collection of stories, like the many memorials in Berlin, is another way of remembering and moving on. The past is not forgotten, but the city has its life in the present and in its ambitions for the future. These are stories, fictions, literary texts—but they come from lived experience, they are knowledgeable, individual, exact. In their different ways they should please and enlighten all readers, those who know Berlin well and those who are new visitors there.

Helen Constantine

Introduction

Berlin gets under your skin. It is not a beautiful city, like Paris, nor an ancient one, but it is fascinating. Since I first went there as a student, Berlin has drawn me back time and again. The appeal of the city lies in its history, of course, but also in the speed with which Berlin reinvents itself. Every time I go back, something has changed—the city never stands still.

The short story is a good form to turn to for a portrait of the changing city. The tales I have chosen for this anthology give snapshots of Berlin through the twentieth century. Since German reunification in 1990, Berlin has grown again as a literary metropolis, and the 1990s and the beginning of the twenty-first century have seen a boom in German short story writing. I have picked a number of texts which are more or less contemporary, although their subject matter reaches further back in time. These stories introduce authors who though well known in Germany may be new to English readers (indeed, many are here translated for the first time into English), and who deserve attention.

Not least, they counter the impression German literature often has abroad of being serious, heavy—and long!

The stories here range in style and tone from fantastic to ironic, polemical and political to poetic, risqué to serious. Many of the texts draw on the tradition of reportage, particularly those from earlier in the twentieth century. Kracauer describes the modern city of the 1920s and 1930s, in the Weimar era, the sheer speed, the new urban perspectives, and above all the bright lights of the neon metropolis; Döblin, at the other end of the city, examines the grimy back streets, poverty, and soapbox politics which are the flipside of that glittering time. Tucholsky's light-hearted sketches about the Berliners in their habits and natural habitat are instantly recognizable more than eighty years after they were written. Banciu meanwhile describes a contemporary encounter with a familiar figure within the city: the busker in the underground.

The short stories of the late 1990s and beyond looked to American writing in particular for a new impetus and lightness of touch—an international outlook which is another example of Berlin's desire and determination to be a world city. (Judith Hermann, a leading exponent of this new deceptively carefree style of writing, is not represented here, though the eponymous short story in her successful and widely translated collection *Summerhouse, Later* evokes a certain Berlin generation in the 1990s.)

Röggla and Draesner translate the sheer speed and globalization into their fast-moving, thrill-seeking characters: their party-goers and internet entrepreneurs embody a new spirit for the twenty-first century, not without irony. Other tales use more conventional story-telling forms. Franck's child narrator is kept in the dark by her mother—the reader may suspect the truth, but what is revealed at the end of the tale turns out to be a different secret entirely. Schley's tale draws us in with a symbolic illness and a medical mystery, where the ending comes unexpectedly.

Berlin has always been a city in flux; the extraordinary changes in Germany's capital since reunification are only the latest redefinition of the city as a twenty-first-century metropolis. When Germany unified in 1871, the new capital Berlin was still largely a collection of villages, as readers of Theodor Fontane's Berlin prose will know. By the beginning of the twentieth century Berlin had transformed itself from provincial town to a modern centre of commerce and politics, 'Chicago on the Spree'. It has only relatively recently become the capital city once more, and home to building works, water pipes, and a sea of cranes. During forty years of division, West Berlin was under the control of the Allied Powers, while the half-city East Berlin was 'Berlin, the capital of the GDR'. The decision to redesignate Berlin as capital after Germany's reunification was not uncontroversial, given the events that had befallen the city during the twentieth century. In the title of Alexandra Richie's history of the city, Berlin is 'Faust's Metropolis': an image which conjures up temptation as well as danger. These two poles have characterized Berlin's twentieth century—the decadence and licentious freedoms of Weimar Berlin (think *Cabaret*) on the one hand, and on the other, the politics of repression under the Nazis, the horrors and destruction of the Second World War (in which around 40 per cent of Berlin was destroyed), and later, the GDR which walled in West Berlin to stop people escaping from the East.

In the light of Berlin's past, the stories in this volume are organized along roughly historical lines. My intention has been to match earlier texts with recent ones, so that historical periods can be seen both from their own time and with historical distance, emphasizing the (often physical) layering of Berlin's history and the continuing presence and impact of the past in the contemporary city. The early twentieth-century Berlin of Kracauer and Döblin leaves traces of decadence in the recent texts: Bach evokes drug-fuelled decadence from the Weimar era, Röggla updates it to the rushing 1990s, Draesner's Gina is a postmodern mix of sex and internet commerce. The ruined and occupied city after the Second World War is painted by Kunert in poignant detail, and the post-war poverty is evoked with pathos in Schnurre's tale. This time also echoes in later texts, as Gröschner's visitors to the neon Sony Centre conjure up the war and Kaminer ironically suggests that Russians reconquer the city as tourists. The Cold War division symbolized by the Berlin Wall—the key event in Johnson's text about the Berlin transport system—is overcome as well as recalled in Maron's memories. Boehning's text by contrast treats the recent past of the GDR era, symbolized by a deserted, forgotten factory building.

History inheres in locations within the city. Döblin's flâneur's account provides evidence of literature's ability to preserve aspects of the past, not least in the many street names around Alexanderplatz that have changed since he wrote the text. Likewise buildings and monuments leave a symbolic mark in these tales as they do in Berlin. Almost wherever you go in Berlin, the TV tower will pop up somewhere in the distance. The spindly landmark is the first thing I look for when I fly into Schönefeld, and my point of orientation on the S-Bahn journey from the airport on the outskirts to the centre of the city. Similarly readers will turn corners in these tales to find landmarks they recognize. The tales evoke well-known locations— Alexanderplatz for Döblin (which provided the title of his famous novel), Potsdamer Platz for Gröschner and Bach. Kaminer refers to the Reichstag, the parliament building with such a difficult past: the fire in 1933 which the Nazis used as propaganda to seize power; Russian graffiti from the end of the Second World War is still preserved in the masonry; and its restoration was begun in earnest after Christo and Jeanne-Claude wrapped it in 1995. Since the Bundestag (the German lower house) has relocated to Berlin, Sir Norman Foster's new transparent cupola has symbolized democracy, but also given tourists a spectacular view over the city. The Kaiser-Wilhelm-Gedächtniskirche, the 'broken tooth' church on the Kurfürstendamm, left in its war-damaged state, turns up in several texts. Recent visitors to the city will no doubt have experienced the neon modernity of the Sony Centre, or seen the long-drawn-out deconstruction of the Palace of the Republic, the uncompromising GDR building which is the focus of Schley's tale. In the late 1990s the emotive decision to dismantle the Palace, possibly in order to rebuild the earlier imperial Schloss, crystallized questions about history and the city: what is to be preserved in the new Berlin? Whose history can remain? Schley's tale mixes the story of this symbolic architecture with family relationships. All of these monuments have resonance beyond the city. Of course, the Wall is what first comes to mind for most people when they think of Berlin, and it too has a ghostly presence in these texts: unspoken in Johnson's depiction of the divided transport system, dismantled in Maron, superfluous in Bach.

Kennedy's famous phrase, 'Ich bin ein Berliner', applies to the many outsiders who have come to the city and felt an affinity with it. As Banciu suggests, 'the true Berliners are the ones who are there by choice', and some of the most interesting contemporary German-language fiction is written by non-native speakers and migrants. In this collection, multicultural Berlin is represented by three authors who have made their home in the city, Banciu, Özdamar, and Kaminer. Berlin has always attracted immigrants, from the Huguenots who sought sanctuary there in the late seventeenth century, through to Polish migration in the early twentieth. Maron, whose grandparents came to Berlin from Poland, says elsewhere that 'a real Berlin family has at least one Polish ancestor, and if they don't, they need to invent one, or otherwise replace them with a Huguenot'. The Turks who came as 'guest workers' during the 1960s have settled in the cosmopolitan city and are now by far the largest minority of inhabitants. Özdamar, who originally came to Berlin to work in a factory, is from Turkey, but rather than write about 'Little Istanbul', the area of Kreuzberg around Kotbusser Tor and Oranienstraße where many families of Turkish origins live, she instead evokes the divided city from an outsider's perspective in a typically idiosyncratic account.

Kaminer, himself a Russian immigrant, depicts with ironic humour the marketing of Berlin to the many Russian tourists.

While the texts span much of the twentieth century, they can only give glimpses into the different areas of the city. Like many big cities, Berlin retains a decentralized, fragmented topography. The short story, with its limited scope, is well-suited to reflect the particularly local character and loyalty of Berlin's districts. Beyond East or West, Berliners belong to their 'Kiez', their neighbourhood, and these texts demonstrate a sense of extremely local pride: Banciu refers to 'her Mitte', Kunert's Platzker takes his street with him into exile, Özdamar's text is simply entitled 'My Berlin', and in the collection from which the tale here is taken, Röggla sings the praises of rundown Neukölln. In Franck's tale by contrast, the child narrator's ignorance of the geography of the other half of the city is a historical indictment of the GDR: on East German maps of Berlin, the Western half remained blank. Perhaps more for the insider are the detailed topographies of Maron's tale, her ultra-precise description of the junction of Invalidenstraße and Chausseestraße, or Röggla's party people arguing about directions through the city at night—should they take the Oberbaum Bridge or Jannowitz Bridge? There is more to Berlin than its architecture and man-made form: Tucholsky and Schnurre evoke the green spaces of the Tiergarten—the location until recently of the famous Love Parade—and the Volkspark Friedrichshain, with its hills made from a million cubic metres of rubble dumped on top of two wartime bunkers.

A map is supplied at the back of the volume, so readers can trace the characters' movements across the city. Berlin attracts trainspotters, perhaps because the BVG, the transport system, seems surprisingly efficient to British eyes (and you can use your mobile in the underground!). I must confess I have had many conversations which revolved around the quickest way of getting from, say, Anhalter Bahnhof to Zoologischer Garten (known to English speakers as Zoo Station), or from Schönefeld to Samariterstrasse. I am not the only one. The transport system has iconic status in the blue-and-white U and the green-and-white S signs that Johnson evokes; and it has been a measure of historical events. Transport—whether on the underground (U-Bahn), overground (S-Bahn), trams, car, or bike—plays a large role in the tales in this collection: journeys within the city, travel for its own sake, are part of Berlin's reputation as ever-shifting, fast-moving. Banciu's text is an evocative account of a Friday night journey on the underground. More poignant are the journeys beyond the city—in Kunert's text Herr D. Platzker leaves Berlin to escape the Nazi regime and returns after the war—or the ones which cannot happen. Johnson's postscript to his famous text about the S-Bahn alludes to the Berlin Wall as the hindrance to free movement across the city. For him, the transport system is symbolic of the wider political and historical situation.

For me, Maron's description of her place of birth sums up the personal relationship that authors and readers alike will have with Berlin. She writes that the city is populated by her, and by her memories. Both the city and the tales here hold associations for me. Like Özdamar's Theo and Kati, I too lived in a flat with only a Kachelofen (the tiled stove typical of old housing stock) for heating, and spent a freezing Berlin winter hauling briquettes to feed the stove. I could go on... This anthology is for all part-time Berliners, who will have their own personal recollections to add to the ones in the tales.

Many thanks are due to Helen Constantine for her careful reading, thoughtful comments and for her patience; to David Constantine for kindly translating the verses by Goethe; and to Karen Leeder for bibliographical help. I would also like to thank the editors, copy-editors, and the marketing, publicity, and art departments at Oxford University Press; and the friends (and fellow *Wahlberliner*) who have supplied photographs.

Lyn Marven

KEMPINSKI HAUS VATERL

Unser Fasching
Suchen
im
HAUS VATERLAND

KAMMER

TÄGLICH 2 4 7 9 UHR

TRAUMULUS

HILDE WEISSNER
HILDE v. STOLZ
HEINZ HÖNIG
HARALD PAULSEN
HANNES STELZER
H. BRAUSEWETTER
CARL FROELICH

LICHTSPIELE

Potsdamer Platz

U

Seen from the Window

Siegfried Kracauer

We can distinguish two types of cityscape: those which are formed deliberately, and others which develop unintentionally. The former derive from the artistic will that is realized in squares, vistas, arrangements of buildings, and effects of perspective which Baedeker generally illuminates with a star. The latter on the other hand come into being without having been planned in advance. They are not compositions like Pariser Platz or La Concorde which owe their existence to a single architectural conception, rather they are creations of chance, which cannot be accounted for. Wherever a mass of stone and lines of streets, whose components result from completely different interests, come together, there you will find this kind of cityscape, which has never been the focus of any interest as such. It is no more designed than nature itself, and resembles a landscape in that it asserts itself unconsciously. Without a thought for how it appears, it slumbers through time.

Outside my window the city coalesces into a view that is as magnificent as a spectacle of nature. But before I turn to that view I should recall the position whence it unfolds. The location is high above an irregular space, which possesses a wonderful ability. This square can go unnoticed, it wears a cloak of invisibility. Situated in the middle of a metropolitan residential area, the point where several broad streets meet, the small square eludes public attention, so much so that hardly anyone even knows its name.

Perhaps this magical skill is due to the fact that the square is primarily used by through traffic. Thousands cross the square every day in the omnibus or tram, but precisely because they traverse it without any fuss, they fail to take any notice of it. And so the square enjoys the incomparable good fortune of being able to live relatively incognito in the midst of the bustle, and although it is open to all sides, it is as if it is surrounded by dense fog.

The cityscape, then, that begins in this small square, is a space of extraordinary expanse, occupied by a metallic iron field. It reverberates with railway tracks. They emerge from behind the wall of a larger-than-life tenement block, from the direction of Charlottenburg station, run in skeins alongside each other and disappear finally behind ordinary houses. A swarm of gleaming parallel lines, which lie so far below the window that the whole sweep can be surveyed at once. With its many signal masts and locomotive sheds the area almost gives the impression of a mechanical model that a boy, kneeling somewhere out of sight, is using for experimentation. His game is to make the delightful, brightly coloured S-Bahn trains slide up and down at a frantic pace, he chases individual locomotives back and forth and dispatches heavy express trains to famous cities like Warsaw and Paris, which are built just around the next corner. The tracks flash, the signals go up and down by turns, and the clouds of smoke linger for a long time. The boy leans contentedly over his work, which is made all the more complete by a noisy tram underpass. It must have been hard to draw the underpass through the whole railway level in such a straight line. But it was worth the effort, for countless wagons whose speed seems to be doubled in a time lapse now run through the tunnel without a thought. The rolling trains on top and, one level below, this running cross-trail of wagons: the trickle never stops for a second and yet never disturbs the peace of the iron plain. It is bounded at the far side by a narrow, pale strip of houses, which breaks it up like the edge of a wood the hastening meadows.

You can hardly tell the windows from the balconies, that is how distant the strip is. The radio tower juts above it, a thin vertical stroke drawn by a pen through a piece of the sky.

In the evening the whole cityscape is illuminated. Gone are the tracks, the masts, the houses—only a single field of light shines in the darkness, such as gives comfort to the night-time traveller because it heralds imminent arrival. Lights are scattered above the space, they hang quietly or move as if they were on strings, and ahead, close enough to touch, is a blinding orange glow which a large garage is using to promote its renown far and wide. A gleaming tree rises up from out of the midst of the tumult, which has no depth: the radio tower, which emits a sphere of light all around its tip. Circling incessantly, the flashing light scans the night, and when the storm rages it flies over the high seas whose waves wash round the field of tracks.

This landscape is Berlin unposed. It has grown un-aided, and without intending to do so, it gives expression to the city's contradictions, its hardness, its openness, its juxtapositions, its glamour. Recognizing cities is linked to deciphering the pictures they speak to themselves while they dream.

East of Alexanderplatz

Alfred Döblin

A sunny morning; I set out to walk around the edges of Alexanderplatz. Otherwise Alexanderplatz with its maelstrom of humanity tempts me so much to head straight to the square itself; for once I wish to get a feel for the periphery of this powerful being. Wide streets, many boulevard-style, lead into it; I approach from the Lichtenberg side. In Frankfurter Allee they have let the green strip of lawn along the middle die off; the street has become completely functional. There are department stores; ready-made outfits for poorer people, plenty of junk too. From the entrance hallway to one house comes singing; people are standing around; I go in. There in the yard a scruffy younger man is acting, gesturing with a comic theatricality, and singing—singing, yes, what? Heil dir im Siegerkranz.[1] All the verses; this is the first time I have heard it since 1918 and I can't believe it. The people giggle, some are embarrassed; he carries on bellowing. And he hasn't misjudged this appeal to sentimentality. As he comes out he apologizes left and right, suddenly he straightens up again: 'Don't get het up. I have to make money, just like everyone else. The workers give me nothing; they have nothing.' A blood-red poster hand on many of the houses: 'You! Are you a fighter in your own cause?' Flyers showing a lifebelt on the sea praise a workers' party. The fly-posting on the houses is a barometer of political agitation; you can see the colours here, so to speak. I stick my head round numerous pub doors; poor attendance. One landlord tells me what I already know: the high prices, and one brewery has sold some of its horses and is apparently switching production to foodstuffs. Which is no bad thing: bread is better than beer. On Strausberger Platz a crowd has gathered outside a newspaper outlet; in the middle a small long-haired youth with an open neck Schiller collar is debating with a calm older worker. The older man says: 'You are protecting the Jews.' The fierce younger boy, with other people's assistance: 'No, we are

---

[1] Prussian anthem, replaced as German national anthem in 1918 after the end of the Kaiserreich.

not defending the Jews. But we know that capitalism lies in class and not race.' It's the first street debate between workers that I've heard to bring up anti-semitism. But no-one took him on; the people have been trained. A newspaper seller is droll; on his stand he has the sign '50% off the cover price to read the newspaper'. People are thronging by a garden fence, I think it must be an accident or a political speech (which is much the same thing). But it is the illustrated crime sheets: they are looking at the mother 'mauled by a bear', and 'an Italian love tragedy'.

Now I turn into Weberstraße,[2] a narrow street. Lots of low houses, all run-down; mortar is falling from their façades. A long stretch of the left-hand side of the street is occupied by carts belonging to small traders; a mass of poor women walk holding children and packages in front of them; there is cauliflower, fat herrings, cheese in boxes, fish on ice, first-rate bulb onions. Over the way is a 'Central Lodgings House'; traders get special prices, they buy and sell stamp paper here. Numerous cellars of products with price lists in front of the door, written in chalk, a 'Purchasing Bureau for Precious Metal' (such pride). A tailor sits in a window display and sews: an 'express tailoring service'. Everyone trades and then buys something else; there is a demand for bags and parcel-string

---

[2] Now part of Linienstraße.

everywhere. In a 'Commission House' wait beer tankards, cut-off telephone books, an easel, a smoking set, military boots. A lending library; a whole window full of brightly coloured trash: 'The Warehouse Thieves', 'Moral Misdemeanours in the Metropolis', the series 'Savage Killers', 'Winoga, The Last Mohican'. The title pictures are captioned: 'A flash, a bang, the big chief sank to the ground', 'There's your reward, traitor'. A serious workers' bookshop; one side of the shop is painted with a hand lying on an open book, with ears of corn and a sickle; underneath 'To produce more you need to know more'.

I cross over Landsberger Straße. On the corner a nice young woman is sitting at a rubber heel seller's; she is sitting in her bare stockings, completely serious; he whets his knife, cuts the heels of her boots into shape; hammers. Gollnowstrasse.[3] The street is darker and crumbling in parts more than Weberstraße. Proletariat and lumpenproletariat. More storage cellars, 'Sorting places'. A coffee shop carries incendiary pictures: 'Wannsee postponed'. A sign shouts: 'You have a treasure and don't know it'; it is a philately shop. The treasure is old letters lying on the floor. Galician types appear; on the other side of Neue Königstraße,[4] in Linienstrasse, there are more of them. There are houses which are epically dirty and fantastically fragile. Undeterred a barber in an absolutely unbelievably

---

[3] Also now part of Linienstraße.   [4] Now Otto-Braun-Straße.

pitiable house promises: 'No waiting! Good, clean service'. Wretched white-bearded men in torn kaftans walk past. Groceries in entrance hallways. The owners stand in front of furniture shops, second-hand clothes stores and scan the passers-by.

Bülowplatz[5] holds the pompous 'Volksbühne' theatre; it is surrounded by deserted storage yards for old iron, rails. Very lively traffic; it seethes with people. And always 'bargains', cloth shops, clockmakers, boots.—Left is Grenadierstraße.[6] Here there seems to be a permanent crowd. The carriageway filled with people; they come and go from the angular, ancient houses. This is a very easterly quarter, guttural Yiddish dominates. The hardly numerous shops have Hebrew signage; I come across forenames: Schaja, Uscher, Chanaine. In shop windows a Jewish theatre advertises: '*Jüdele der Blinde*, five acts by Joseph Lateiner'. Jewish butchers, craftsmens workshops, bookshops. People are moving in unceasing flurry, looking out of windows, calling, gathering in groups and whispering in dark hallways. On one corner everyone is standing around a good Berlin crier, an Eulenspiegel: a white mouse runs over his cap, he displays artworks with fake million Mark notes, and goes on to sell soap: 'Clear water, gentlemen, that's the best proof.'

---

[5] Now Rosa-Luxemburg-Platz.   [6] Now Almstadtstraße.

I clear a path for myself. Wind my way through to Münzstraße. Pass the cinemas which play continuously in broad daylight, with fairground organs which clamour over the street: they tempt you with 'Marko, the Man of Strength', and 'The Fate of a Decent Woman'. A stream of people, of traffic; Alexanderplatz is near. Between numerous very cheap women, searching among the hurrying folk, wander strangely slow individuals who obviously know each other, recognize each other, step to the side, carrying small suitcases. Lingering here and there. Lots of idle youths with cheeky caps. The Alexander constabulary barracks arrives, the endlessly long building belonging to the Tietz department store; it makes a new, rather cute corner. Then the broad expanse, green grass, Alexanderplatz, the Salvation Army field kitchen, surrounded by curious faces and lines of the old and poor, the dark red police headquarters.

Evenings after Six

Kurt Tucholsky

Blessed whoever, hating none,
Shows the world the door,
Heart to heart then with the one
Friend alone to share
The joys of things nobody knows
Or thinks of as they might
That down the labyrinthine ways
Of feeling walk the night.

Unknown poet[1]

[1] In fact these verses come from a well-known poem by Goethe, translated here by David Constantine.

Evenings after six the Berlin Tiergarten is full of people walking, arm in arm and with their hands clasped in front as well—they are all in the right. This is how:

He picks her up from work or she picks him up. The couple stretch their legs for a bit, after sitting down for so long in the office the evening air does them good. Along the grey streets, through the Brandenburg Gate, for example—and then through the Tiergarten. What do they do while they walk? They tell each other what has happened during the day. And what has happened during the day? There have been annoyances.

Now admittedly, as the phrase would have it, they should 'swallow their annoyance'—but that isn't true. People don't swallow anything. At the time they can't answer back—not to the boss, not to their colleagues, not to the porter; it is not advisable, the other person gets a higher salary, so they are in the right. But it all resurfaces later—evenings after six.

The lovers wander through the green pergolas of the Tiergarten, and he tells her what things were like at work. First the report. You may have already noticed how the battle reports of such conflicts are given: the person reporting is a shining example of calm and goodness and it is only the evil enemy who has gone raving mad. It sounds roughly like this: 'I say Herr Winkler, I say—it won't work, doing the filing like that!' (This in the calmest voice in the world, mild, serene and wise.) 'He says, "Excuse me!" He says, "I will file things as I see fit!"' (This fast, incoherent, and wildly choleric.) Now the High Command again: 'I say quite calmly, I say, "Herr Winkler," I say—"we can't just file things like that, because otherwise the C-post will get mixed up with the D-post!" And then he starts to yell! he wouldn't take orders from me, and he would certainly not do what other people told him to—doncha think—?' Of course both parties were actually as loud as fishwives. But sometimes it was the boss, and they can't answer him back. So they 'swallowed it'—and now it explodes. 'Doncha think—?'

Lottie thinks it's scandalous. 'Hah! You see!' That feels good, that is balm for a suffering heart—finally they can get it all off their chest!—'What I would have really liked to say to him is, do your stuff yourself then if you don't like it! But I won't stand there in front of such an ignorant individual! The bloke doesn't understand anything, I tell you! Hasn't a clue! The way he does it now he'll definitely get the C-post in with the D-post—that's a dead cert! Yeah, well I don't care. I know what to do anyway: I'll leave him to do it himself—then he'll see how far he gets!' A shyly admiring glance over at the giant hero. He is in the right.

But she has something to report too. 'The way Elli schemes, you wouldn't believe it. Fräulein Friedland had on a new blouse the day before yesterday, and she said on the phone, we overheard it—"We know where some colleagues get the money for blouses from!" What do you think of that? But Elli doesn't have a fiancé herself any more! Hers left a long while ago—off to Bromberg!' A quarrel, a fight with the second floor all along the line—in the thick of the fight. 'I didn't say anything...but I thought to myself: well—I thought, we know where you get your silk stockings from too! Do you know, she is picked up every other evening, she always gets the car to wait round the corner...but we found out straight away! She's completely shameless!' He squeezes her arm and says: 'Fancy that!' And now she is in the right.

That's how they wander. They stroll along, the many many couples in the Tiergarten, telling each other things, pouring out their petty sorrows to each other, and all of them are in the right. They restore the balance to life. It would simply be unhealthy to go home in that state: with all the pent-up annoyance from the conflicts of the last nine hours. It has to come out. Inaccurate bills, stupid phone-calls, answers missed, rude remarks restrained— they all come out into the open. The *esprit d'escalier* of work stories has a field day here. The blue veil of dusk settles on the trees and bushes, and the interlocked couples walk the paths and kill their bosses, destroy the opposition, shoot the enemy right through his false heart.

The audience is grateful, attentive and boundlessly credulous. It applauds incessantly. It shouts: 'encore!' at the best parts. It kills, destroys and shoots along too. It is comrade-in-arms, friend, brother, and public all at the same time. It is nice to perform for this audience.

Evenings after six businesses are reorganized, employees promoted, bosses dismissed, and, above all, salaries fixed. Who would set different rates? Who would calculate the bonuses justly? Allocate holidays with bonuses? The couples, evenings after six.

The next morning everything starts afresh. They go to work even-tempered, yesterday's irritation has gone, been shaken off, hats and coats hang in the closet, books are rearranged—well then! The rows can begin. At three o'clock on the dot they come—the same story as yesterday: Herr Winkler doesn't want to file the post, Fräulein Friedland wrinkles her nose, the holiday list has a gap, and the bonus isn't in sight. Annoyance, fat head, pointed conversations on the phone, gloomy silence in the office. There's a storm brewing. The thunder growls. The refreshing rain only comes later in the evening—with her, with him, arm and arm in the Tiergarten.

There is peace on earth and goodwill to the lovers, the accused has the last word—and they are all in the right, every single one of them.

Just a Sec—!

Kurt Tucholsky

Berliners, wherever they might find themselves left on their own, will stare at the floor and suddenly jump up, as if they have been bitten by a tarantula: 'Where can you make a phone call round here?'—that fact is well known. If Berliners didn't exist, the telephone would have invented them. It is their master, and they are its creations.

Picture a bold young man, who is attempting to interrupt a serious businessman during an important transaction. He won't succeed. Halberds block the way, private secretaries throw themselves across the threshold, he will have to tread on their private parts to get past, and every attack the young man makes, however bold he may be, is bound to fail. Unless he telephones.

If he telephones, he can disturb the president in parliament, the chief editor doing corrections, madam while she is trying things on. For in Berlin the telephone is not a piece of mechanical equipment: it is an obsession.

If people are knocking threateningly at the door, a Berliner wouldn't think to open it. But if a small apparatus rings, he will dismiss with a wave even the most aristocratic visitor, murmuring with that obsequious expression you only otherwise see on pious sectarians: 'Just a sec—!' and full of keen interest he will throw himself at the black receiver. Forgotten are business, the midwife, stock exchange and insolvency negotiations. 'Hello? If you please? This is—who is speaking?'

Talking to a Berliner for fifteen minutes without being disturbed by a phone call is an impossibility. How many punchlines fall flat! How much collected energy simply goes up in smoke! All in vain, cunning negotiations, spite, and underhandedness, however beautifully figured-out! The telephone is not the invention of Messrs Bell and Reis—Vischer with a V[1] put all the object's spite into a casing. It only rings when you don't want it to.

How often have I experienced a guest's voluble speech convincing the entire room that he's nearly made it, victory is near, hurrah, just one more step... then the telephone rings and everything stops. The fat man at the desk, who a moment ago, almost completely mesmerized, had

[1] Friedrich Theodor Vischer (known as Vischer with a V because of the spelling of his name), writer of satirical plays particularly.

let his double chin sink onto his cravat and peaceably pursed his lower lip, lets an icy mask slip over what he passes off as his face. With a nervy hand on the telephone, he forgets his partner, business, and himself. 'Dinkelsbühler here—who is speaking—?' He whirls energetically in the unknown water, completely caught by the other speaker, unfaithful to his partner of only a minute before, entirely surrendered in deceit and betrayal.

It is the other person who is the idiot. He just sits there, hollow and empty, the pathetic words he has only just spoken hang senselessly from his mouth like an old flag in the Zeughaus,[2] the standard of a regiment which has long since died. He sits there humiliated, adrift, and naked, and his unfulfilled will seethes silently inside. What now?

Now the fat man at the desk talks for as long as people talk on the phone in Berlin, and there is only one other person who talks more: the person who is on the other end of the line. He must be thundering like a medium-sized waterfall: the man at the desk gazes thoughtfully at some blotting paper, his gaze travels over the inkwell, he stares confusedly and vacantly at his betrayed partner's bald spot, then he starts to doodle stick men and squares on the paper, and the person on the other end, as the

---

[2] The old arsenal, on Unter den Linden; now the site of the Deutsches Historisches Museum (German Historical Museum).

croaking earpiece announces, seems to be sending whole dictionaries' worth of words roaring through the telephone.

Soon the guest starts to shift impatiently on his seat, then the unending conversation shows the first signs that an end is near. 'Well then . . . !'—'So let's leave it at that . . .' The guest starts to feel happy: just as the concert-goer's soul hurries on ahead to the cloakroom when the orchestra gets threateningly loud, when the conductor's flapping throws more and more brass into the bluster . . . but it isn't over yet. They stay like that for a while, making ever more concluding remarks, the conclusion itself doesn't come. Gradually the person waiting develops a desire to hit the person on the telephone over the head with the codebook of commercial law . . . 'Well then—auf Wiedersehn!' he says eventually. And hangs up.

And that is the worst moment of all. The lights behind the man at the desk's eyes change, you can actually hear things click as he reconfigures himself; with a rather moronic expression he turns back to his old, betrayed partner, squinting. 'So—where were we?'

Now start from the beginning again. Pick the shattered pieces of your conversation up off the floor, take a deep breath, make an effort to find the train of thought again . . . Good night. The momentum has gone, the joke has gone, the will has gone. The discussion limps to an end. You have achieved nothing. And that's what the Lorelei has done with her singing.[3]

Now the reader will put the book down quietly and amicably and think about this for a moment. Then he will jump up like a hunted stag, the *Mona Lisa* smiles on the ground... He rushes to answer the telephone.

[3] A line from Heinrich Heine's famous poem, 'Die Lorelei'.

...uller?

Brita+Ursel

+Krista...

Wo seid Ihr?

Meldung hinterlegt

bis 27.11. mittags Du

Krupp-Gaststätten,

Tiergartenstr 30t;?

sonst fahrt nach K.

Melchior

Am Fasanenhof

7.1

Everyday History
of a Berlin Street

Günter Kunert

They finished building it in October nineteen hundred
and two: that's when its life begins, staid and almost
colourless, in the light of the hissing gas lanterns, under
the auspices of a still not dull sun; only later does the
smoke grow and grow.

Its real history begins with a jolt: in January nineteen
hundred and thirty three, with Herr D. Platzker, who is
not a Herr gentleman, just a person and by no means
characterized by his name, and certainly not by his job,
which he gives as 'technologist'.

Everything else is determined by the fact that
D. Platzker does not wait for the end; for the end of a

speech that another man holds, whose job is master of the *Volk*, an anti-person in fact, who in contrast to Platzker is sufficiently identified by his name. You know who I mean.

This speech talks—volubly, but yet very indirectly— about D. Platzker, what is more, it is threatening. And even as the gigantic, bloodthirsty words are still tumbling out of the moustachioed mouth, Platzker is at home hiding about his person his toothbrush, a small amount of money, for want of a large amount, and finally the most important earthly piece of any person: his passport.

His hat pulled down over his face, he steps out onto the street, finished in Oct zero-two. He sees the street lying there, poor but rich in promise, the same as a hundred others and quite unique, and he can't bring himself to abandon it to a future as dark as the inside of a coffin. In one go, with the aforementioned jolt, he simply picks it up. Rolls it up, as if he were rolling a carpet, bends the roll in the middle and stows it under his coat. After all: he's a technologist. Unfortunately he loses a few inhabitants in the process, amongst them the old lady from the tobacconist's, without a trace, and all the birds over the rooftops, mid-flight and mid-screech.

As he crosses the border, the street is lying under his seat; at the border control they don't pay any attention to it, they are looking for more valuable things, they take off

Platzker's coat and peer under his hat and unmask the D Full Stop in front of his name as David and the reason for his departure. But they don't stop him fleeing in the face of disaster. In any case: every Goliath is most powerful on his own.

On the other side of the border the journey can slow down a bit, it stretches out and expands, soon it reaches beyond Europe, and fades away somewhere distant. So distant that we can't even obtain any specific details about the material conditions of Platzker's existence there. Even he himself will never be entirely sure where he ended up and what was really around him. That stems from the fact that he is swiftly interned, as a German spy, or anti-German, or both, whereupon he loses contact with the ethnological particularities of what surrounds him before he has actually had a chance to make contact.

On the other hand his alienation from his surroundings is because of the street, which he brings out immediately after his arrival in the camp, one icy day, in order to wrap himself up in it on top of his coat, which works only too well. He discovers its preventative effect against rigours of the most unpleasant sort; that's what makes it so strangely beautiful, the inexplicable, alluring, dangerous beauty of ugliness. David Platzker is entirely absorbed by it. Nothing can reach him when he's immersed in the ornament on the houses' façades, in the apparently indifferent expressions of the false cupids, the cement caryatids, in the expressions of the plaster gargoyles, which become more ambiguous day by day and come to resemble the faces of the street's inhabitants. When the weather is dull the features on the faces of the living and the stucco ones shut down, as if they're wondering what has brought them so far from the city they call home. But when the sun breaks through and a wandering finger of light brushes over them all, they light up like hope itself. Then the curtains are pulled to one side, full-bosomed figures appear in the windows and can be seen shaking the beds; or in rooms in semi-darkness, where wine-red wallpaper can just be made out, movements hint at naked bodies.

The posters do not change, advertising the same things on the *Litfaßsäule*[1] year after year; the men do not change, their perennial blue-enamelled tin canisters in their hands, on the way to work or on their way home; the girls' breasts don't change, they steadfastly remain girls. The dull panes light up punctually in the evening. With a swishing noise the lamps on the pavement spring to life at their set time, to spread a moderate light around.

At such moments Platzker throws himself onto his straw bedding and the street under his campbed, whence he brings it forth time and again.

---

[1] Round column on the street for bill posters and adverts.

This is the only way to explain the fact that he doesn't know exactly how much time he has spent in the Hörselberg[2] of the camp when he hears about the end of that man who was the reason he left; and then the end of the war and with it, most importantly, the end of his internment. He is sitting in the ship already, or the train, or the suburban line before he actually becomes aware that he is nearly home.

He wanders round the remains of the city, and it takes an age before he finds the district where he used to live. His intention is to lay the street back down where he had taken it from—after all, it doesn't belong to him. In any case, the city has a lack of intact streets, and they could really do with this one he has brought back.

By certain traces which have survived near the Frankfurter Allee, which is his point of orientation, he recognizes the exact spot where the street belongs. When no one is looking, he takes it out, carefully unrolls it and spreads it out among the singed brickwork in the area. It won't go back in though, however he pushes it and adjusts it. It doesn't fit any more.

Platzker hasn't a clue what he should do with the street; he was only a kind of custodian for it for a

---

[2] Real mountain in Thuringia, associated in myth with the devil and occult practices.

while. He doesn't feel he is authorized to keep it. And because he is only a person, and somewhat timid where such unbelievable things are concerned, he thinks that if he could give it back untouched and safe, he might possibly be contributing to this rather vague and fuzzy notion of 'conciliation'; he might even be thanked for it.

With a heavy heart he leaves the street lying where it is, and walks back to his hotel. In the night he can't sleep. A void surrounds him, uniform darkness. Loneliness. He misses the street.

The next morning, after having taken the difficult decision during the night, he goes bright and early to the Frankfurter Allee and comes across the traces which mark the spot. Chalk messages shout from the pock-marked plaster: WHERE IS ERNA? WE'RE ALIVE! THE CHILDREN ARE...

Rubble grows in piles, with iron girders poking out, unidentifiable bars with colourless scraps fluttering from them. Platzker keeps looking round for his street, until he realizes he has been standing in it for a while. The window frames are empty, no naked forms, no full-chested figures, no figures moving behind them at all. The only thing standing motionless behind the open rectangles is the formless sky.

David Platzker gently leaves the street that once possessed him—or he it. There's no way of telling which any more. As he walks away, his foot kicks against a blue enamelled canister, which rolls away, spilling a liquid which looks like fresh blood.

The Loan

Wolfdietrich Schnurre

Father generally went to a lot of trouble at Christmas. It was admittedly particularly difficult at that time to get over the fact that we were unemployed. Other festivals you either celebrated or you didn't; but Christmas was something you lived for, and when it finally came you held on to it; and as for the shop windows, they often couldn't bring themselves to part from their chocolate Father Christmases even in January.

It was the dwarves and the Kasperles[1] that did it for me particularly. If father was there, I would look away; but that was more conspicuous than staring at them; and so gradually I started to look at the shops again.

Father was not insensitive to the shop window displays either, he just hid it better. Christmas, he said, was a

---

[1] Puppet theatre clown, similar to Punch.

festival of joy; the important thing now was not to be sad, even if one didn't have any money.

'Most people,' father said, 'are just happy on the first and second days of Christmas, maybe again later at New Year. But that's not enough; you have to start the being happy at least a month before. At New Year,' father said, 'you can feel free to be sad again; for it is never nice when a year simply goes, just like that. But now, before Christmas, being sad is inappropriate.'

Father himself always made a big effort not to be sad around this time of year; but for some reason he found it harder than I did; probably because he no longer had a father who could say to him what he always said to me. And things would definitely also have been much easier if father had still had his job. He would even have worked as an assistant lab technician now; but they didn't need any assistant lab technicians at the moment. The director had said that he could certainly stay in the museum, but for work he would have to wait until better times.

'And when will that be, do you think?' father had asked.

'I don't want to upset you,' the director had said.

Frieda had had better luck; she had been taken on as a kitchen help in a large pub on Alexanderplatz and had also got lodgings there straight away. It was quite pleasant for us not to be with her constantly; now we only saw each other at lunchtime and in the evening she was much nicer.

But on the whole we didn't live badly. For Frieda kept us well supplied with food and if it was too cold at home, we went over to the museum; and when we had looked at all the exhibits, we would lean against the heating underneath the dinosaur skeleton, look out the window or start up a conversation with the museum attendant about breeding rabbits.

So actually it was entirely fitting that the year be brought to an end in peace and tranquillity. That was, if father hadn't worried so much about a Christmas tree. It came up quite suddenly.

We had just collected Frieda from the pub and walked her home and lain down in bed, when father slammed shut his book, *Brehm's Life of Animals*, which he still used to read in the evening, and called over to me, 'Are you asleep yet?'

'No,' I said, because it was too cold to sleep.

'It's just occurred to me,' father said, 'we need a Christmas tree, don't we?' He paused for a second and waited for my answer.

'Do you think so?' I said.

'Yes,' father said, 'and a proper, pretty one at that; not one of those wee ones that falls over as soon as you hang so much as a walnut on it.'

At the word walnut I sat up. Maybe we could also get some gingerbread biscuits to hang on it as well?

Father cleared his throat. 'God—,' he said, 'why not; we'll talk to Frieda.'

'Maybe Frieda knows someone who would give us a tree too,' I said.

Father doubted it. In any case: the kind of tree he had in mind no one would give away, it would be a treasure, a treat.

Would it be worth one mark, I wanted to know.

'One mark?!' father snorted through his nose scornfully, 'Two at least!'

'And where is this tree?'

'See,' father said, 'that's just what I'm wondering.'

'But we can't actually buy it though,' I said. 'Two marks: where could you possibly get that money?'

Father lifted the paraffin lamp and looked around the room. I knew he was wondering whether there was anything else he could take to the pawn shop; but everything had already gone, even the gramophone; I had cried so much when the fellow behind the grille had shuffled away with it.

Father put the lamp back down and cleared his throat. 'Go to sleep now; I'll have a think about the situation.'

The next few days we simply hung around the Christmas tree stalls. Tree after tree grew legs and walked off; but we still didn't have one.

'Could we not—?' I asked on the fifth day, once we were leaning against the heating in the museum underneath the dinosaur skeleton again.

'Could we what?' father asked sharply.

'I mean, should we not just try to get a normal tree?'

'Are you mad?!' father was indignant. 'Maybe one of those cabbage stalks that you don't know afterwards if it's supposed to be a sweeping brush or a toothbrush? Out of the question.'

But it was no good; Christmas was getting closer and closer. At first the forests of Christmas trees in the streets were still well stocked; but gradually they developed clearings, and one afternoon we watched as the fattest Christmas tree seller on Alexanderplatz, Strapping-Jimmy, sold his last little tree, a real matchstick of a tree, for three marks fifty, spat on the money, jumped on his bike and cycled off.

Now we did begin to feel sad. Not very sad; but at any rate it was enough for Frieda to furrow her brows even more than she usually did and ask us what was up.

We had got used to keeping our troubles to ourselves, but not this time; and father told her.

Frieda listened carefully. 'That's it?'

We nodded.

'You're funny,' Frieda said. 'Why don't you just go to the Grunewald forest and steal one?'

I have seen father outraged many times, but never as outraged as he was this evening.

He went pale as chalk. 'Are you serious?' he asked hoarsely.

Frieda was very surprised. 'Of course,' she said, 'that's what everyone does.'

'Everyone!' father echoed, 'everyone!' He stood up stiffly and took my hand. 'You'll permit me,' he said, 'to take the boy home first before I give you the answer that deserves.'

He never gave her the answer. Frieda was sensible; she played along with father's prudery and the next day she apologized.

But it didn't make any difference; we still didn't have a tree, never mind the stately tree father had in mind.

But then—it was 23 December and we had just taken up our usual position under the dinosaur skeleton—inspiration struck father.

'Do you have a spade?' he asked the museum attendant, who had nodded off next to us on his folding chair.

'What?!' he yelled with a start, 'Do I have a what?!'

'A spade, man,' father said impatiently, 'do you have a spade?'

Yes, he had one.

I looked up at father uncertainly. However he looked reasonably normal; only his gaze seemed a touch more unsteady than usual.

'Good,' he said then, 'we'll come back to your place tonight and you can lend it to us.'

It was later that night before I discovered what he had planned.

'Come on,' father said and shook me, 'get up.'

Still drowsy I crawled over the bars of the bed. 'What on earth is going on?'

'Now listen,' father said and stood in front of me, 'stealing a tree, that's bad; but borrowing one, that's okay.'

'Borrowing?' I asked, blinking.

'Yes,' father said. 'We're going to go to Friedrichshain park and dig up a blue spruce. We'll put it in the bath in some water at home, celebrate Christmas with it tomorrow and then afterwards we'll plant it back in the same place. Well?' He gave me a piercing stare.

'A fantastic idea,' I said.

Humming and whistling we set off; father with the spade on his back, me with a sack under my arm. Every now and then father would stop whistling and we sang in two-part harmony, 'Deck the Halls' and 'The First Noël the Angel Did Say'. As always with such carols, father had tears in his eyes and I too was in a very solemn mood.

Then Friedrichshain park appeared before us and we fell silent.

The blue spruce that father had his eye on stood in the middle of a round flowerbed of roses covered in straw. It was a good metre and a half tall and a model of regular growth.

As the earth was only frozen just under the surface it didn't take long at all before father had exposed the roots. Then we carefully tipped the tree over, put it roots first into the sack, father hung his jacket over the end sticking out, we shovelled the earth back into the hole, spread straw over the top, father loaded the tree onto his shoulder and we went home. Here we filled the big tin bath with water and put the tree in.

When I woke the next morning father and Frieda were already busy decorating the tree. It had been fastened to the ceiling with string and Frieda had cut a selection of stars out of tinfoil which she was hanging on its branches; they looked very pretty. I also saw some gingerbread men hanging there. I didn't want to spoil their fun; so I pretended I was still asleep. While I did, I thought about how I could repay them for their kindness. Eventually it occurred to me: father had borrowed a Christmas tree, why shouldn't I also manage to get a loan of our pawned gramophone for the holidays? I acted like I had just woken up, admired the tree in seemly fashion, and then I got dressed and went out.

The pawnbroker was a horrible person, even the first time we were there and father had given him his coat. I would have happily given him something else too; but now it was necessary to be friendly to him.

I also made a great effort. I told him a story of two grandmothers and 'especially at Christmas' and 'enjoying the old days one more time' and so on, and suddenly the pawnbroker struck out and clouted me one and said quite calmly, 'I don't care how much you fib otherwise; but at Christmas you tell the truth, got it?' Then he shuffled into the next room and brought out the gramophone. 'But woe betide you if you break anything! And only for three days! And only because it's you.'

I made a bow, so low that I nearly bumped my head against my kneecap; then I took the turntable under one arm, the horn under the other and ran back home.

First I hid both bits in the wash-kitchen. I did have to let Frieda in on the secret, for she had the records; but Frieda kept mum.

Frieda's boss, the landlord of the pub, had invited us for lunch. There was impeccable noodle soup followed by mashed potato and giblets. We ate until we were unrecognizable; afterwards in order to save coal we went to the museum and the dinosaur skeleton for a while; and in the afternoon Frieda came and collected us.

At home we lit a fire. Then Frieda brought out a huge bowl full of the leftovers of the giblets, three bottles of red wine and a square metre of Bienenstich,[2] father put his volume of *Brehm's Life of Animals* on the table for me, and the moment he wasn't looking I ran down to the wash-kitchen and brought up the gramophone and told father to face the other way.

He did as he was told; Frieda spread out the records and put the lights on, and I fixed the horn and wound the gramophone.

'Can I turn around yet?' father asked; when Frieda had switched the light off he could stand it no longer.

'Wait a second,' I said, 'this damn horn—I can't get it to stay put!' Frieda coughed.

'What horn do you mean?' father asked.

But then it started. It was 'O Come Little Children'; it crackled a bit and the record obviously had a scratch, but that didn't matter. Frieda and I sang along and then father turned around. First he swallowed and rubbed his nose, but then he cleared his throat and sang along too. When the record was finished we shook hands and I told father how I'd managed to get the gramophone.

He was thrilled. 'Well!' he kept on saying to Frieda and nodded at me as he did so, 'well!'

---

[2] Bee-sting: a cake with honey topping.

It turned into a very lovely Christmas evening. First we sang and played all the records through; then we played them again without singing; then Frieda sang along with all of the records on her own; then she sang with father again, and then we ate and finished the wine and after that we made some music; then we walked Frieda home and we went to bed too.

The next morning the tree stayed standing in all its finery. I was allowed to lie in bed and father played gramophone music all night and whistled the harmony.

Then, the following night, we took the tree out of the bath, put it in the sack, still decorated with tinfoil stars, and took it back to Friedrichshain park. Here we planted it back in the round rose bed. Then we stamped the earth firm and went home. In the morning I took the gramophone away too.

We visited the tree frequently; the roots grew back again. The tinfoil stars hung in its branches for quite a while, some even until Spring.

I went to see the tree again a few months ago. It's now a good two storeys high and has the circumference of a medium-sized factory chimney. It seems strange to think that we once invited it into our one-room flat.

Postscript on the S-Bahn

Uwe Johnson

I learnt the Berlin S-Bahn by the lines it sent out to travellers outside the city. Time and again, when the stocky carriages rattle along next to the mainline trains, in Hohen-Neuendorf or at the interchange Grünauer Kreuz, you could see homesickness coming to an end on the faces of the Berliners in the compartment. For them the S-Bahn was the first welcome to their city, now they were back home, it was Berlin from here on. And it was the S-Bahn that introduced the immigrant to the city. The S-Bahn carried him from the mainline stations into the urban provinces, with radiating spokes and a giant ring, and so it furnished him with a spatial conception of the Berlin region, before releasing him out in Köpenick,

or Friedenau, or, unfortunately, Marienfelde. That was
before, when the S-Bahn also held the disputed cities of
Berlin together, when Baumschulenweg was next to
Köllnische Heide and Staaken next to Spandau.[1] Now
the ring is broken. The suburban lines, the city's invitation
to the towns, to Potsdam, Oranienburg, Königs Wuster-
hausen, have been cancelled. In the middle of the
city tracks end in buffers, real, genuine, actual railway
embankments have been cleared away, and no outsider
believes us when we tell them a transport system used to
run over such pointless mounds of earth. If that isn't
enough, we can show them an ex-territorial platform in
the middle of East Berlin, where we change from the
North–South direction towards the West, but where our
friends, possibly on the next platform, cannot go, and
even our view of them is blocked. The S-Bahn must do
its best to remind us of the city's situation. But it has
remained a part, a living member belonging to the city,
even to the half-city. It is not only that we miss the railway,
and the S-Bahn has to make up for it with half an hour's
worth of the feeling of journeying from one fence to
another, on the double benches of old. Now, as then, old
and new Berliners recognize each other by the fact that
they don't talk about the city line when they are sitting in

---

[1] Adjacent stations before the Wall went up, and since reunification.

the circle line, and anyone who doesn't know the difference between the Zehlendorf and the Wannsee branches must be from outside. The S-Bahn is one of our intimacies. It is ours, the puzzling over the peculiar old shades of paint going round the trains, the dark carmine, the ox-blood red, the stolid yellow on top. We recognize the sound without thinking, the rattling passage, the respiring brakes and approach at night, the singing acceleration. The green neon signs on the bridges and stations, the white S: Stadtbahn: it belongs to us, we know where we are. The broad platforms are part of the scenery in the city, and we are awaited there. We are used to the platforms, so we preferred it when they called out the stations and the train's departure rather than dispatching over the radio. We take liberties there to the point of rebelliousness, they want to dissuade us from smoking and we still smoke. The S-Bahn, its cast iron posts, its greenhouse stairs, its out-of-date enamel, keep the city's past in our memory. And we see it all the time, and from its windows we see the city: a window seat here is still worth having. There are people who want to get rid of the S-Bahn. There are others who want the old times back again and, more sensibly, a time with tickets from everywhere, which state not just Berlin East or Berlin West, but Berlin S-Bahn. The choice is quite simple.

Place of Birth: Berlin

Monika Maron

It was on a very warm spring day forty-three years ago that I first thought that I love the city where I was born and in which I have spent almost my entire life. I was in the 46 tram going towards Friedrichstraße, and just after the bend from Invalidenstraße into Chausseestraße, as I was looking through the back window of the last wagon at the hot asphalt on this ugly, war-damaged junction, a feeling came over me that I can't explain to this day, a feeling of disquiet and delight in equal measure, for which the only appropriate word is love. I looked at Chausseestraße's filthy asphalt skin, and thought I wanted to embrace it, wanted to lie down flat on the street with my arms out wide and embrace the street, the city. At the time I was living for a year in Dresden, where I was working as a cutter in the Klotzsche aircraft plant. Almost every weekend I would hitchhike to Berlin. Why this particular moment in the tram at the corner of Invaliden- and Chausseestraße has stuck in my memory as my declaration of love for Berlin, I can't say. I was probably more unhappy than happy at the time, so my silent outpouring of emotion can hardly have been an expression of world-encompassing *joie de vivre* extending even to the ugliest spots, but rather of recognition and of belonging to what I recognized. I had never been able to imagine not being a Berliner, but being from Leipzig or Greifswald instead, or even from Eberswald or Hohenselchow. Not having been born in a capital city was a second-class destiny, I thought, even when the city was capital of a ridiculous state. I never reproached the city for having fallen into the hands of the barbarians who let it deteriorate and disfigured it; after all, the city fared no differently than we did. If Berlin had been a person, it would have been one of us, and not one of them.

When people ask whether I like living in Berlin I usually answer 'I come from Berlin', and usually the questioners are satisfied with that answer. Either they assume that everyone who is from Berlin necessarily likes living in their city, or—which would show their understanding—they know that in such cases the question can only end in paradox, like asking whether you like being your parents' child, because you either are what you are, or you aren't.

In 1988 I moved to Hamburg and for the first time I was living in a strange city without any intention to return. It was early summer and Hamburg was very beautiful with its white houses, sprawling rhododendron bushes, the promising jangle of anchoring yachts, with the many bridges over the canals of the Alster, and I was happy to be living in such a beautiful city. The image of grey, nightmarish, crumbling East Berlin sank under Hamburg's grandeur like a pile of rubble collapsing in on itself. But yet I can still remember precisely the odd feeling of suddenly, aged forty-seven, living in a city where the streets did not hold any memories for me and where the illuminated windows did not mean anything to me. The city was empty of me, which on some days was intoxicating and on others frightening.

Berlin on the other hand is populated by me. In Berlin I could, if I took the notion, come across myself a hundred times a day, at all ages, happy or crying, alone, in company, in love, out of love, I can sit down anywhere and wait for me to come along. I would only need to wander along Schönhauser Allee on a summer night, around four in the morning, and I could see me, rather drunk, next to a young man, I can't remember which one, taking a bottle of milk from one of the delivery crates in front of a grocery shop, not without leaving the money in the bottle's place, and drinking it as I walked. It had rained during the night. The street under my bare feet is warm and slippery with rain-wet dust. My sandals are hanging from the index finger of my left hand. If anyone were to ask me what my favourite places in Berlin are, I would have to say Schönhauser Allee, on a summer morning around four, between Stargarder- and Milastraße. But who would understand?

I can meet myself on the Monbijou Bridge in front of the Bode Museum in all seasons. I am leaning against the bulging railings or sitting on the steps, smoking a cigarette and looking west over the Spree at the flashing Fewa advert on the bridge between Friedrichstraße railway station and Schiffbauer Damm: the red-blue-and-yellow neon outline of a round woman with a bun, washing clothes in a tub and sending little soap bubbles up into the air. I have just been to the theatre, on my own, I saw *Galileo* for the fifth time, or the *Good Person of Sechuan* (second row, standing place for fifty pfennigs), I feel like one of the chosen ones, because I have seen *Galileo* for the fifth time or the *Good Person of Sechuan*, because I held out for four hours or more standing up, because I am alone, most of all because I am alone. I am seventeen or eighteen or twenty and I know that everybody is on their own in life.

On the other side of Unter den Linden, in Hausvogtei-platz, was my school, the Berliner Gymnasium zum Grauen Kloster, later known as 2. Oberschule Mitte, a brick building which looked like a prison, with classrooms arranged around a courtyard, next door to St Joseph's Catholic hospital, from where a disgusting fishy smell would seep into our classrooms every Friday. It's break time now, small groups stand at the edge of the play-ground, groups of boys, groups of girls, most of them walk slowly in a circle around the yard. I can't find me, I'm ill or skiving the last lesson and am sitting instead with a friend on the steps of the Spree, where we are talking about love or the theatre. Her mother works at the theatre, some of the glamour reflects on her, and a dull shine on me, too, when I talk to her about the theatre.

Two minutes' walk from the school was the Niquet-Cellar, which we called Nicki-Cellar,[1] and where Napoleon was once supposed to have made a stop. In the dingy light that the lead windows let into the room from outside I find myself at a table in the corner on the right with another friend. We have the same first name. On the table

---

[1] Nicki means velour, usually for clothing.

there is a small, flat paper bag with six cigarettes, Jubilar brand, which you can buy individually. We are drinking pop and wondering what we could order to drink if we were out with a boy. Pop is embarrassing, we don't like the taste of beer. My friend says she recently ordered coffee. We think coffee seems right.

Shortly after my time at school, when the whole of the Fischerkiez had to make way for high-rises, the Niquet-Cellar was deported to the Taubenstraße and was renamed Niquet-Cell, because it was no longer in a cellar. But that doesn't exist any more either.

Lots of things don't exist any more. It's an effort to remember the old Alexanderplatz, even when I see it on postcards. It was once a proper square, criss-crossed by innumerable dangerous trams. There, where the old market hall used to stand, right by the entrance, I meet myself holding my Aunt Maria's hand, she is buying me a bag of red crayfish, five pfennigs each. I don't want to eat the crayfish, I want to play with them. It's summer, shortly after the war. That came back to me thirty years later when I had to buy my son a pig's foot which *he* wanted to play with.

As the years go by the beauty fades from the pictures. Or perhaps I only noticed its absence as the years passed. Where would the beauty have come from back then?

From the rubble? From the post-war poverty? Perhaps from peace, which I was of course only just coming to know. The question of what I might have thought life was, if the war had lasted for twenty or thirty years, as happened subsequently in Vietnam or the Middle East, and if I had died before it ended, that's a question that has occupied me for a long time. Would I have believed then that life was war? Or might I still have sensed what peace was? And how is someone who has never seen a beautiful city supposed to know what a beautiful city looks like? In that case, something which is more beautiful than something else is beautiful. A city half-destroyed by bombs is more beautiful than a city completely destroyed by bombs. Ruins which have trees growing from them are more beautiful than ruins which don't have trees growing from them. Maybe that's it.

Later, once I had an image of what a beautiful city was, which I got from books, films, because I had seen Prague and Budapest, I had to admit that my city was many things, large, interesting, surrounded by countless lakes and pretty countryside and inhabited by an infamous people, but it wasn't beautiful, indeed not even before it had been crippled by bombing. As the ruins disappeared, transformed into green spaces and parks or replaced by new builds, the memory of the untouched city finally lost its purchase, and what hadn't been destroyed by the war fell into disrepair in peacetime, at least in my part of the city, in the East. Unsound balconies were torn down, broken street clocks disappeared one day and were never replaced, the plaster on the houses discoloured grey and black over time, or fell onto the pavement in large chunks, every winter tore holes in the streets, which were only patched up in summer. You could believe that at some point the pavement in Schönhauser Allee might suddenly open up and simply swallow all the people, cars and trams on the street.

The border between East and West Berlin ran under the S-Bahn bridge in Wollankstraße in Pankow. I only dared to cross it once, in full view of the other people who were walking east or west through the bridge and who could have recognized me. As my parents' child, I was not allowed into the West and was even excluded from leafleting with the FDJ.[2] I hide behind the turned-up collar of my coat, my heart is beating so loud that I'm afraid that the policeman who checks the identity card of every third or fifth or seventh person to cross the border can hear it. What do I want to do on the other side? I watch as I hastily walk into the West, past the stalls of tat towards Badestraße, and disappear in the sea of people.

[2] Freie Deutsche Jugend (Free German Youth), the official GDR youth movement.

In 1961 the bridge became part of the Wall. The last side street before the border is called Schulzestraße on the right, and Brehmestraße on the left-hand side. The sides on the west of both streets belonged to the East, and were out of bounds and could only be entered with permits. The view onto the grounds of the S-Bahn behind the houses required permission from the authorities. In the mid-eighties, when I was allowed to travel for a year, I visited a schoolfriend of my mother, who lived on the western side just beyond the bridge. It took me an hour and a half to go on the tram to Friedrichstraße, from there to Wollankstraße on the S-Bahn, and to end up where I had set out in Pankow: more precisely, ten metres beyond Pankow. I am standing up on the platform and can see into Schulzestraße where my friend K lives, on the eastern side. I hope that she will come out of the house at this moment so I can wave to her, but she doesn't come. I turn around and look at the West, where Wollankstraße simply continues, which I had almost forgotten.

A year later, in November, I can meet myself at the bridge for the third time. I am standing in the middle of a group of forty or fifty people with a stupid beatific look on my face and watch as the workers dismantle the Wall with pneumatic drills and other machinery. 'Nothing more will happen today,' one of the workers shouts to us. We all stay put, we don't want to go through the bridge, we could go via Bornholmer Straße or other crossing points which are already open if we wanted; we want to see the end of the world being carried away, metre by metre. Most of the onlookers are the same age as me, and also watched as the street and all the destinations to which it led disappeared behind concrete. The man next to me with a child on his shoulders smiles at me, I smile back. Everyone who catches someone else's eye smiles at them. I know some of the people standing around, others seem familiar. It doesn't matter who we are and what we have done in our life before now, in this moment a boundless happiness unites us. For anyone who hasn't experienced that, the S-Bahn bridge in Wollankstraße, under which the districts of Wedding and Pankow adjoin, is a shabby, ugly place, which you only enter in order to leave it quickly with your next step.

Our mythical memories have their roots in beginnings, hence so often in childhood and youth, when everything is a beginning and nothing is everyday, when every day still brings a first, first rubber, first book, first stilettos, first concert, first cigarette. I have been living in Schöneberg for ten years, but the most enduring images I have of West Berlin come from the time when the Wall was still standing. I am crossing Tauentzienstraße at Wittenbergplatz, I stop on the central reservation in the middle of the road and look right, just trying to spot a gap between the cars going past. It's late afternoon or early evening in autumn, the windows are already lit up, at the other end of the street the Gedächtniskirche asserts its symbolic importance. Like a black sentinel it dominates the picture, and I think that the street, the light, the church are not there for me, that I don't belong in this picture, because my visa runs out on the first of October. I didn't actually go until the second of October, which we, that is, all of us who were sitting at my friend E's kitchen table that evening, drowning our melancholy in wine, christened the MSO, the Memorable Second of October. In Spichernstraße underground station, where we were the only people waiting for the last train to Zoo station, I sang for the others one more time their favourite song of mine; although I was far too hoarse from the smoking and drinking and talking loudly in the pub, I sang through the echoing station the song of the silent youth, in Russian: Na zakate khodit pa-a-ren ... [3]

And I can remember vividly an earlier night during a car ride through Kreuzberg when I suddenly caught sight of a junction which was the identical twin of a junction in Prenzlauer Berg and then I thought I recognized Warschauer Straße and really understood for the first time in fact that the two halves of the city were part of

---

[3] 'As the sun goes down, a boy walks...'

a whole, that their parts belonged to the same body. At night, when darkness swallowed the colours and the grey-black contours of the lines of the streets and the silhouettes of the houses were all I could make out in the dark, the city revealed what had remained hidden from me during the day under the restored façades and bright billboards, and behind the magnificent arrangements in shop windows.

In the meantime the severed connections between the two halves have long since been reconnected and the centre of the city belongs to everyone once more. But still when I cross over one of the lines where the Wall used to stand a strange feeling comes over me.

Although my flat and my restaurant of choice are located in the West, and most of my friends who also used to live in the East live there too, the eastern part of Berlin will probably always be more familiar to me. Why I choose to flee this familiarity rather than seek it out, that I might know in another ten years. I don't believe any of the answers which occur to me at the moment.

Cities where I have spent a few days or weeks have left behind images in my memory, impressed on me moments which are stored like photographs. Berlin by contrast is a space, a large, half-lit room through which smells and

sounds drift; first here, then over there, suddenly illuminated, scenes appear and dissolve again, voices ring out,
clear and unreal like in a dream, they are drowned out by
uninvited noises, till they fall silent. I can't tell which rule
governs my remembering. Apparently at random and
unexpectedly the walls bounce back a faint echo of my
life, audible only to me.

Family Friend

Julia Franck

My father is lying in bed.

'Where is mama?' I ask him. He yawns, groans and pulls the cover over his head. The bed next to him is empty.

'She's in the bathroom, making herself beautiful,' my father murmurs into the covers. I leave him in peace, he often works nights and then we are considerate during the day. In the bathroom stands my mother, the toothbrush sticking out of her mouth, she is brushing her long black hair.

'Can I?' I ask and stand on my tiptoes to reach her arm and the brush. I love combing my mother's hair, it's thick and heavy like a horse's mane. I can imagine that I am stroking her fur, my hand nearly reaches the brush. But my mother lifts her arm higher and says we don't have time. My mother is wearing a lilac-coloured nightdress. I like all the colours that my mother likes. I sit on the edge of the bath and try to touch the wall opposite with my bare toes.

'Stop that,' says my mother, 'you'd better put some socks on, it's cold, and do you want to wear that skirt?' I nod, it's my favourite skirt. She keeps forgetting, she has so many things to think about of course. My mother likes thinking lots and sometimes sighs when I interrupt her and want to tell her something myself. Then I wait until it seems to be a suitable moment. My mother shakes her head, gathers her hair and puts it up. She bends over to me and opens the tap on the bathroom stove. The water streams onto the yellow sides of the bath. Steam rises, the heat smells salty. My mother takes her t-shirt off and I say to her that she looks like Morgan striding through the mists of Avalon.

'Shift along there,' my mother says and pushes my knee so I move over a bit on the edge of the bath. She crouches in front of the stove and opens the little iron door. She leans forward, blows and lights a cigarette on the glowing embers. She blows again. The briquettes flicker. I hold my nose. My mother laughs and says I should get myself out of there.

The whole floor in the children's room is strewn with paper cut-outs. Yellow, red, black. My sister Hanna is sitting on the carpet, she is chewing on her stuck-out tongue and picking a yellow scrap from my flag with great care.

'Don't!' I yell.

'Yes,' she says, 'if you take it off it's a West flag.'

'You shouldn't do that,' I say to her.

'It looks stupid anyway,' she claims, 'you can't even see what it is.'

The doorbell rings.

'I'll go,' Hanna calls, drops my flag and jumps up. I shove Hanna out of the way as I catch up with her just before the door. Standing outside is Thorsten who laughs at us. He opens his arms wide, but we don't want to jump into them, at least I don't, because he has his fur jacket on again, and anyway he only comes when we want to do something with our mother.

'Mama is in the bath,' I say to Thorsten.

'And Papa is sleeping,' Hanna says.

'I see,' Thorsten comes in the door, 'then I'll make coffee and wait until she's finished, do you two want anything?' He pats me and Hanna on the head. We follow Thorsten into the kitchen and show him where the coffee is.

'I want cordial and water,' Hanna cries, she jumps onto Thorsten's lap. Thorsten pours cordial into a glass for Hanna and asks me if I want some too. I shake my head.

'We don't have any time today,' I inform Thorsten and now his lap is occupied I would rather look and see what my mother is doing and when we can set off. As I come into the bathroom she is just washing her armpits. Her breasts are covered in bubbles, so you can't even see her nipples.

'Should I rinse you off?' I ask my mother, but she wants to do it herself because I always soak everything straight away. She dries herself off and asks if Papa is still sleeping. Of course. 'Then we'll let him sleep, he'll be happy if he gets a bit of peace and quiet.' My mother slips into her red velvet dress and puts lipstick on. She has a dark red lipstick that my father likes very much and I do too. My mother is the prettiest.

'Should I comb your hair?' I ask.

'Oh, no,' my mother laughs and undoes her hairclip, 'it's fine as it is.' Her hair falls over her shoulders and reaches nearly down to her waist. Maybe I should tell her that Thorsten is sitting out there in the kitchen and I don't want him to come with us. But my mother would pretend not to understand, because she's known Thorsten for ever and is happy when he comes and always laughs in a funny way when my father says to her that the family friend has been there again and left a note on the door. And then my father smiles too. We have lots of family friends but Thorsten has been coming here just too often recently and I wonder if I should say something to my mother some time, after all she might not have even noticed, she always has so much to think about that she doesn't see some things at all. Like she even forgot to send us to bed yesterday evening and we were able to play until one in the morning. My mother squirts something onto her wrist.

'What is that?'

'Opium.' She laughs secretively and whispers: 'From Uncle Klaus in the West.'

'You smell lots better without perfume,' I say to my mother. She strokes my head and pushes me out the door in front of her. In the kitchen she creeps up to Thorsten and puts her hands over his eyes and he pretends he doesn't know who it is. Then she bends over him and presses her face against his. I can understand very well why Thorsten comes to visit us often.

Thorsten says he's brought something for my mother. He presses something into her hand. I really want to see what it is, but she doesn't want to show us. She laughs and takes a sip of coffee from Thorsten's cup.

'Can we?' he asks. My mother says to us, 'Shush shush, put your shoes and jacket on and say bye-bye to Papa, but do it quietly.'

I ask my father if he doesn't want to come with us, everyone is out on the street for the First of May and they're celebrating, even the People's Army is coming and

Erich Honecker[1] and everyone has red carnations and is happy, and we made flags in school weeks ago, after all even Thorsten is coming too. Hanna blows her triola. Can't he hear the drums? 'Come,' I say, and try to pull the covers away. No, my father wants us to go on our own so he can sleep a bit. My mother comes in, kisses my father on the neck and whispers something to him in his ear, he hugs her and I try to get in between their arms, I hug my father too until he says he can't breathe but I don't let go of him, he tickles me on the tummy and the arms and just everywhere. Hanna shouts, 'Me too, me too.'

I would like to stay with my father, but my mother says we should be considerate and leads me and Hanna out of the room. Before she shuts the door I can see my father flinging the covers over his head. He must be glad that we're going finally.

Thorsten is standing in the hall and offers Hanna his shoulders. I take my mother's hand, in my other hand I'm holding the flags.

In the S-Bahn I want to look out the window and want my mother to sit next to me. But she doesn't want to, she is whispering with Thorsten and then they speak Russian so we don't understand.

[1] Erich Honecker took over from Walter Ulbricht as General Secretary of the SED and leader of the GDR in 1971.

'You always have to be so secretive,' says Hanna. Thorsten and my mother laugh at us. My carnation comes off its stalk again and I try to stick it back, till Thorsten takes it out of my hand and reckons he can make it whole again. But he doesn't manage to and gives me his instead.

We change at Alex.[2] Hanna and I would like to stay there. There are children bathing in the fountain, and we want to bathe too. But our mother says we'll go to Thorsten's first, the Stabil building blocks that we like so much are there too. We would rather go to the music with our flags and be where all the other people are. Our mother promises that Thorsten has coloured puffed rice at home.

Thorsten nods, and says he also has cordial. We don't have any choice anyway. But that doesn't mean I'll take Thorsten's hand, I only want my mother's. My mother is wearing her fur coat, although it's already warm and she is sweating. At the station I crawl under her coat. My mother smells good. Hanna tries to feel my head through the coat, and I stick both my fists out so she mistakes them for my head. We take the U-Bahn and get out after a few stops.

Thorsten's flat is small and it smells. That's the rubbish bins, Thorsten explains and points down into the yard.

---

[2] Alexanderplatz.

I think it's Thorsten's fur jacket, but of course he won't admit it. Hanna and I get a bowl of puffed rice put in front of us on the kitchen table. We divide it out according to colour. Red is my favourite colour, green is hers. Thorsten takes my mother's hand and pulls her into his big room and closes the door. Hanna wants red to be her favourite colour from now on, I have to choose another one. She's stupid, there's no way I'll do that, red was always mine, I can't change it now. We can hear mother and Thorsten giggling. They didn't really need to close the door for that. Hanna is boring, she doesn't want to play. We want to go now. I go to the door that mother and Thorsten disappeared behind. It is jammed, I try the handle several times but the door won't open.

'Mama!' I call. Behind the door it is quiet. Hanna comes over and presses against the door.

'Won't open,' I say.

'Mama!' Hanna shouts louder now. Behind the door it stays quiet. I kick the door with my foot and rattle the handle, Hanna beats her fists against the door and gaily shouts in time, alternating 'Mama! Thorsten! Mama! Thorsten! Mamathor stenma mathorstenma ma!'

Then we hear steps and the door flies open. I fall on my knees and Hanna falls over me.

'Why do you shut the door then?' I ask when our mother laughs and says we should stand up. She is standing in the middle of the room, and Thorsten, who opened the door for us, sits down on the bed. He puts a sock on.

'We want to go now,' Hanna says, and jumps on Thorsten's lap. Thorsten asks my mother if she could give him his shoes, and she picks up the shoes from under the table and brings them to him on the bed.

'I'll put your shoes on, okay?' Hanna offers, she drops backwards from his lap and hangs upside down, and tries to put his shoes on like that. My mother needs to go peepee, I follow her. She says I should wait outside. At home I'm always allowed in with her.

'We'll eat something first,' my mother decides when she comes out of the bathroom. She would like to cook risibisi.

'Oh nooo, I thought we were going to the First of May.'

Thorsten says you can't go to the First of May, it's a day and not a place or a person. Thorsten always knows better, that's why he's also quite stupid. I don't want to be at Thorsten's. Every time we're at Thorsten's my mother wants to stay there and often it gets very late before we can go. We have even had to sleep at Thorsten's because it turned into night and there were no more U-Bahns running.

My mother stands at the cooker and fries onions. She says we will have a surprise this evening and so we need to have eaten properly. Thorsten puts a flat box down on the floor and says we can play with his Stabil building blocks now. But I don't want to and Hanna doesn't either.

'What kind of a surprise?' I ask my mother.

'A surprise is a surprise,' she says and starts to sing. Thorsten is standing next to my mother and sniffs her hair, then he says something quietly to her that I can't understand.

'Thorsten doesn't need to do that,' I whisper in Hanna's ear. Hanna turns round to the two of them.

'I think Thorsten likes Mama,' Hanna whispers back.

'So what, that doesn't mean we have to stay in his flat all day.' I hold my nose and pretend I'm going to vomit. Hanna agrees. Although I'm not sure that she doesn't secretly like him just as much, after all she always jumps straight on his lap when my mother isn't sitting on it.

We have to come to the table and eat, otherwise there won't be any surprise.

'So what, I don't care,' I say and cross my arms. Thorsten is playing airplanes with Hanna, he's feeding her, but she isn't a baby any more.

'What are you looking like that for?' he asks me.

'I'm not looking like anything,' I tell him and turn my back on him. Now it's dark outside and we haven't been at the First of May. Thorsten makes me really angry, he just doesn't understand anything.

'Now don't fight,' my mother rolls her eyes.

I say to her, 'Don't be so nervy.' That's what my father always says to her too. She doesn't react, instead she asks Thorsten where the cigarettes are. Thorsten lights one and passes it across the table to my mother. The two of them stare at each other.

'What's up?' I ask, I want to go home. No-one answers. The doorbell rings. Thorsten puts the fork in Hanna's hand and goes to the door. A friend of Thorsten's has come. My mother, the friend and Thorsten stand in the hall and talk quietly to each other. Surprises are stupid, really stupid, really really stupid. I tell my mother that too, when she comes back into the kitchen.

'Just eat up first and then we'll go.'

I chew the rice and peas, roll each one round on my tongue until my mother shouts at me to behave normally for once, I'm just impossible. Her voice stretches apart strangely, like on our record player when Peter and the Wolf got deeper and deeper voices and my father said that the motor wasn't running fast enough any more. Hanna has also got a deep voice. She has laid her head down on her arms and is pretending to sleep. I need to yawn.

'Hanna,' I say, and my tongue is very heavy. Thorsten looks like he's in a house of mirrors. We were in Treptow, with the rollercoaster and Thorsten had a silly laugh like that there too, really silly, very silly. I push my plate away and lay my head on the table, my mother's hair is hanging in my face. It sways back and forth. I feel my mother's arm, she lifts me up, she's going to carry me to Thorsten's bed, I don't want to sleep there. But she carries me even further and my tongue is such a lump that I can't say to her how stupid I think it is and I can't cry either because my eyes are so heavy.

The air is stuffy, it smells of cigarettes and is dark. Something drones and shakes. I try to make out what. There is something heavy lying on my chest, I clutch at it, it's Hanna's arm, she is still asleep. In the front I hear my mother's voice, she says we have to turn off to the left here. The car motion is making me feel slightly sick. I didn't know that Thorsten had a car. I close my eyes again. That's good, I think, he can drive us home again in the evenings then, even if there aren't any U-Bahn trains running.

The rain patters on the car roof, I see a small dashing stream of water flowing over the window. Every time another car goes past it hisses.

'I'm thirsty,' I say. My mother turns round to look at me, she strokes my head.

'So you're awake again, hm?' She passes me back a bottle. In the bottle is pop, Astoria, I think, but the bottle looks different. I think, it doesn't matter, I'm dreaming. I find it odd that I can think about dreaming in a dream. But the niggling in my arm shows I'm not really sleeping much. If my arm is asleep and I notice that, I can't be sleeping properly myself.

'I feel sick,' I say to my mother.

'Oh it'll pass.' She strokes my forehead, like I'm ill. Thorsten looks over his shoulder and asks, 'Slept well eh?'

Slept well? I screw up my eyes and only open them again when I'm sure that Thorsten isn't looking back any more.

'When will we be home?' I want to know. My mother doesn't let go of my forehead.

'When will we be home?' I push my mother's hand away, she ought to give me an answer finally.

'How late is it?' my mother asks.

'Half four.' Thorsten lights another cigarette.

'We'll be a little bit longer, go back to sleep okay?' My mother imagines that's easy. Now we are driving through streets, I can see streetlamps going past outside. We stop at traffic lights. There are yellow road signs and I try to read what is on the signs. Tempelhof, Marienfelde.[3] No idea where that's supposed to be. I close my eyes and try to sleep, I feel sick. I can feel my stomach, I sit up again and need to vomit. My mother tried to hold her hands up but most of it went in between the two front seats. I cry, because the acid in my mouth tastes disgusting. My mother gives me the pop again and asks me if I don't

[3] In West Berlin: Marienfelde was the location of the refugee camp for people fleeing or leaving the GDR.

want to take off my blue neckerchief, I could clean myself up with it.

'Are you mad?' I say to my mother, it's my pioneer scarf, but apparently my mother doesn't care about pioneer scarves, just as she doesn't care about the First of May and the fact that my father will already be worrying where we are.

My Berlin

Emine Sevgi Özdamar

In 1976 I returned to Berlin after nine years. After the military putsch in Turkey I had ended up in the hands of the police. My friends Theo and Kati in Berlin had mobilized Amnesty International to fetch me to Berlin. They lived in the first floor of a villa in Steglitz. Kati's mother lived below them. Kati said, 'You can stay in her flat for a week. She's at a health farm.' The flat was cold, there was no central heating, just a *Kachelofen*.[1] 'My mother hasn't had proper heating installed,' Kati said. 'She thinks the Russians will come anyway, why should I have heating put in for the Russians.' Kati and Theo were Young Socialists.

Between 1965 and 1967 I had already lived in Berlin and had returned to Istanbul with two records of Brecht's

[1] A tiled stove.

Songs by Lotte Lenya and Ernst Busch. Then in Istanbul I attended the Drama School and listened to these songs over and over again for years. My grandmother would listen with me and ask, 'What are they singing?' I translated *'Und der Haifisch / der hat Zähne / und die trägt er im Gesicht'*[2]—'I hope the shark doesn't get into paradise,' she said. She was expecting to go to paradise herself you see, because eight of her children had died. 'On the Day of Judgement I will stand on the bridge between heaven and hell. This bridge is as thin as a hair and as sharp as a sabre. If the sins were too great, the bridge cuts the sinner in half, and he falls down into hell. But because my eight sons and daughters died when they were just children, they hadn't yet sinned and now they are angels. They will come flying and lift me off the bridge onto their backs and take me to heaven.'

When I left this time, Grandmother said to me, 'You will come back in a few days won't you? When I'm dirty you'll wash me again won't you?'

'Grandmother, don't cry, don't cry!'

'Look, I'm not crying, but please come back again in two days!'

When my grandmother next needed a bath I was sitting in the train to Berlin. I had left behind many

---

[2] The first lines of Mack the Knife, 'Oh the shark has pretty teeth dear / And he shows them pearly white' (in the 1954 Marc Blitzstein translation).

friends who had been killed. For one young man who had been hanged there would be no more evenings, no cat, no cigarettes.

At Zoo Station I waved to all the buses going past. I was in freedom and was pleased about the rain. I thought, Berlin has waited for me for nine years. It was as if back then when I returned to Istanbul Berlin had frozen like a photo, to wait for me—with the long, tall trees, with the Gedächtniskirche, with the double-decker buses, with the corner pubs. Berliner Kindl beer, the crosses on the beer mats. Walls. Checkpoint Charlie. U-Bahn. S-Bahn. Cinema on Steinplatz. *Abschied von gestern* (Yesterday Girl). Alexander Kluge. Bockwurst sausages. The Brecht theatre Berliner Ensemble. *Arturo Ui.* Canals. The Peacock Island. Tramps in the stations. Pea soup. Lonely women in Café Kranzler. Black Forest gateau. Workers from different countries. Spaghetti. Greeks. Cumin-Turks. Café Käse. Telephone dances. Bullet holes in house walls. Cobblestones. Curried sausage. White bodies waiting for the sun at Lake Wannsee. Police dogs. East German police searchlights. Dead train tracks, grass growing between them. House notices: 'In the interests of all residents children are forbidden to play games.' Stations left behind in East Berlin which the West Berlin underground trains pass through without stopping. A solitary East-policeman on the platform. Solinka soup. Stuyvesand cigarettes.

Rothhändle cigarettes. Signs: 'Achtung Sie verlassen den Amerikanischen Sektor / Warning you are leaving the American sector'. Jewish cemetery in East Berlin. Ducks on Lake Wannsee. A bar with music from the 1940s, old women dancing with women. Broilers.

I had known a Turkish opera singer in Istanbul, she had loved Berlin very much. She had studied singing in Berlin as a young woman, she particularly liked singing *Tristan and Isolde*. When she got pregnant in Berlin and had a difficult birth, the Berlin doctor said to her, 'Try Isolde's aria.' So her daughter, who later became my best friend, came into the world to it. She too was an actress, we worked at the same theatre in Istanbul. In her identity card it said Place of Birth: Berlin. During the military dictatorship I had often looked at her identity card, 'Place of Birth: Berlin'. From Zoo Station I phoned the Brechtian actor and singer Ernst Busch in East Berlin. 'Are you really Ernst Busch? I heard your voice every day for nine years. Can I see you?'—'Come, just arrange a time with my wife.' I was happy and thought I was flying.

Later I worked at the Volksbühne theatre at Rosa-Luxemburg-Platz as Benno Besson's assistant. So during the day I lived in the theatre in East Berlin and at night I went back to West Berlin to Kati and Theo. Every time I came out of the underground I was surprised, 'Ah, it snowed in the West, too. Ah, it rained here, too.'

One night when I had come back from the East to Kati and Theo's villa too late, I could only open the door to the building, but not the door to the flat. So I slept in the stairwell. The next morning Theo tripped over me, 'Kati you locked the door again, Sevgi couldn't get in!'—'Sorry,' Kati said, 'sometimes I get up in my sleep and lock the door twice. I don't know why, but I think sometimes I'm also afraid of the Russians, like my mother.'

Later I got a one-off three-month visa from the GDR authorities. So I didn't have to exchange money every day, but in return I wasn't allowed to go back to West Berlin for three whole months, otherwise the visa would have been invalidated.

Before I moved to East Berlin I walked through West Berlin once more and read the writing on the houses and the Wall: Why are you all so desperate . . . Everything we have forgotten screams for help in our dreams . . . God is dead, the executioners aren't . . . We don't need tear gas, we already have plenty of reasons to cry . . . GDR: German DRoss . . . Achtung! You are entering the Axel Springer sector . . . Reds for the gas chambers . . . Time to live—got to go to work first . . . USA-Army go home . . . Shame concrete doesn't burn . . . Die Deutschland . . . People wake up—better shake up the state . . . Death to mediocrity . . . Women strike back . . . No riots without demolition . . .

I loves ya... Being a cop, that's top... Fire & flames for this state... Learn peace... Germany shut your mouth...

I said to the *Volkspolizist* at the border, 'I have a three-month visa for East Berlin'—'For the capital of the GDR,' he said.

I stayed with an actress who learnt Spanish in her kitchen every morning and didn't know if she would ever get to see Spain. She reckoned that she would go there as a pensioner in forty years. I said to her, 'Karl May went travelling in his own room too.' The names of the stops for the Volksbühne made me happy every time: 'Rosa-Luxemburg-Platz'. I liked the U-Bahn station 'Marx-Engels-Platz'.[3] In Turkey people had been put in prison because of books by Marx, Engels and Luxemburg. I also liked the fact that cucumbers cost the same in every shop: 40 Groschen. In contrast to West Berlin there was no writing on houses or the Wall. Above some old shops you could make out faded words:

Firewood—Potato peelings. Fine cookware. Cut pageboys, perm. Pickled cabbage. Coffins at all prices. Repairs carried out professionally.

Heiner Müller, who worked as dramaturge at the Volks-bühne, said: 'In the East words have much greater impact than in the West.' He translated *Hamlet* for Besson. At the

---

[3] An S-Bahn station, now Hackescher Markt.

line 'Something is rotten in the state of Denmark' during the premiere the East Berlin public began to laugh. But after a few people had whispered 'Ssh!' it went quiet. Heiner said, 'They know that the play will be banned if they laugh too much. So they don't laugh, they have an agreement among themselves not to laugh.'

Sometimes on a Saturday or Sunday I went to Friedrichstraße station. That's where the trains stopped in which West Germans sat, and then they carried on to West Berlin. Here even I really began to long for the West. I called Kati. 'Is it snowing where you are too?' When the trains had departed, the people went back into the station bar, but they came up again immediately the next train came which was going to the West with its doors that had to stay shut. Down below in the station there was a cigarette kiosk. One of the brands was called 'Speechless'.

In the theatre canteen an actor told stories about getting out. Once a man had tried to flee to the West as a swan. He made himself a swan's head, put it on and swam through the Spree. The real swans came over to him, pecked at his fake swan head and swam with him to the West.

I walked from the station to the cemetery in Chausseestraße. There some of the gravestones lay like giant books on the ground. I always went to Bertolt Brecht's gravestone. He had made specifications for his gravestone himself. It was to be a simple stone, 'which every dog wants to piss on'.

On his grave had grown the same flowers that my grandmother always used to plant in Turkey. KÜPELI (with earrings). On the gravestone was written: 'He made suggestions and they were carried out'. Near Brecht was the grave of Heinrich Mann, on which I often saw an East Berlin cat sitting. In the evening I had a dream. I found myself in a large, crooked room. Brecht was lying in a bed. I said to his wife Helene Weigel, 'I want to speak to him'—'But he is dead'—'No, he is not dead, he is just sleeping. Please, give me something of his. His tie or his pillowcase.' Weigel gave me Brecht's pillowcase.

Then suddenly I found myself on the steps of a moving ship.

Behind me were standing fascists from Turkey.

And Hegel lay there, his gravestone was red granite. One time I came across an eight- or nine-year-old boy at his grave. He said to me, 'Georg Wilhelm Friedrich Hegel wanted to be buried next to Johann Gottlieb Fichte. Fichte died of typhus, Hegel died of cholera.' From Hegel's grave I went to Brecht's, the boy came too and I sang quietly '... *Und der Haifisch, der hat Zähne...*' Then I said to him, 'My grandmother was scared that the shark

might get into paradise.'—'Where do you come from?'—
'From Turkey.'—'Where is Turkey?'—'Near Bulgaria.'

We sat a while by Brecht's grave. Then the boy wanted
to accompany me to my flat. When we were standing in
front of the house, he said to me,

'My father has an atlas. When I'm home I will ask him
to show me where Turkey is.'—'Perhaps we'll see each
other again.'—'Yes, I come to the cemetery at 2 o'clock
on Saturdays.'—'See you on Saturday.'

Squatters

Inka Bach

The sun has risen over the Landtag.[1] The sun moves in the direction of Schöneberg, soon stands next to the Staatsbibliothek library. Men and women emerge from the S-Bahn-shafts at Potsdamer Platz, walk en masse down Leipziger Straße to the Treuhand[2] in the Haus der Ministerien and the Gauckbehörde[3] in Mohrenstraße, make for the Gropiusbau, form thin dark lines on the grass between the Esplanade and the Weinhaus Huth on the way to Potsdamer Bridge. Then no-one around for hours until late afternoon; only occasional individuals looking for something, lost, in the no man's land. After 6 o'clock Potsdamer Platz is a dead island. But cars move

---

[1] The old Prussian Diet, now seat of the Berlin state parliament.
[2] The institution charged with selling off GDR industries after reunification.
[3] Repository for Stasi files.

day and night across the spider's web around what was once Berlin's intersection.

The waste land is opened up in October 1994. Midges which had crawled from their larvae undisturbed for forty years swarm up in swaying black clouds next to the linden trees that used to line the street, flee into the Weinhaus Huth, threaten to overwinter there. At the end of November they are still pestering soles of feet, ankles, backs of hands, and cheeks during the night.

By day it is cool and sunny. The sky is unusually high this autumn, the clouds draw sharp edges. The Platz is not just another empty, desolate place, it stretches out like a desert since the first holes began to gape. The marquee for the foundation stone ceremony is being taken down. It still reflects the sun on its roof like a giant pane of light. And then it is gone. Construction phase 1 can begin.

Between the Landwehrkanal and the Staatsbibliothek the excavations for the construction go ten metres deep. At intervals of half a metre a drill sinks into the sandy soil, silicon is left in the earth to seal off the hole from the ground water, which is still lapping around on the surface at the moment. Not far away the U-Bahn flies up out of the ground, twists onto the elevated track and clambers its way to Gleisdreieck. The only road across the Landwehrkanal has been laid for the construction lorries, it stretches out in a straight line, bare all the way to Potsdamer Platz. On the grounds of the building excavations the cement mixer set up on site turns sand into concrete.

The yellow digger scoops muck and more muck in its jaws. Guddling, the Berliners call it. More than ten years ago she lived by the motto: make love in ruins, die on building sites!

One morning in December 1983. The woman, four men. A house, fourth floor. A couple. They are awake early. He came to her briefly, went to work at half six. She is reading.

The flat they live in had been occupied by a thirty-year-old architect before them. Rumour has it that she was also a prostitute and drug addict. Some people thought she was mad. But maybe she was just on her own too much in the big flat. She pulled down a supporting wall, which the squatters later had to prop up. She jumped out of the window. She left behind a mountain of stones in the kitchen and a pile of diaries, all the same grey-brown books in A4 format, possibly bound by hand. They carried the stones downstairs. They couldn't decipher the diaries.

Gradually it gets light. The sound of the sirens carries from Winterfeldtplatz. Always the police. But easy, today it might not be for them. A minute later they are in the yard.

'Achtung, Achtung, this is the police!' The hard mega-phone, her heart beating hard. Eviction, the eviction. She jumps out of bed, runs to the window. 'Winterfeldtstr. 31 is being searched by order of the court.'

Searched, just being searched. There have been more than a dozen house searches already. But the pounding heart every time. There are only two of them in the house today, the other three men are at work. It will soon be Christmas. 'Do not leave the house! Have your identity cards ready!' They have to get dressed quickly, then they go back to the window. It won't be long before they are here on the fourth floor. She shuts the window, it's too cold.

House searches were more amusing in the summer. Back then she had calmly started to clean the windows. It was a joke for the others. Someone threw her cigarettes. Others kept supplying the people who were already stand-ing in the yard with cherries. Summer made them strong and merry. The cold is dreadful though.

Policemen in green are standing in the stairwell, on every landing there is a state-employed Christmas tree. They are freezing like the squatters. They are in a bad mood. Boring, their job. Boys, they are younger than the squatters. No hate. No fear. Just bored in their cold posts. Waiting and looking through the plate glass in the staircase.

Now the doorbell rings. Two civvies are outside the door, detectives, men with gravitas. 'Come here please!' Leads her. Inspection of the flat. Polite. Aggressive. They only look around briefly. They are just the ones who have been sent on ahead. Their colleagues will come later. A quick glance into each room. The beds have not been made. Then the last and biggest room: the library. Now they are curious. They go closer. Too many books. Now they are tough. 'Well someone here has a lot of money.' They are only looking at the books at eye-level. 'We like reading,' she shouts to them from the doorway. Her anger grows. Wordlessly the two detectives take in the red and white striped shelves, the boards from the building site. One of them plucks at the battered leather sofa. 'Real horsehair!' he declares. Just go! but she controls herself. The squatters broke through the wall to the next apartment two years ago, they were thinking about May 68 in Paris. A passage, out of sight of the detectives. 'There's clearly no vacuum cleaner here.' The fact they are dirty and lazy, that's the worst they can come up with. 'If you give us advance warning next time we'll clean up for you.'—'Yeah well, it doesn't bother me.' She holds the door open for them, says have a good day. The policeman standing outside peers through the crack in the door. 'Auf Wiedersehen.'

Is it perhaps an eviction after all? Don't wait. 'Come on, we'll play dominos instead.' They play dominos on the kitchen table. Doorbell. The next moment, with no in-between, someone is kicking the door. Which opens under the force of the boots. The Christmas trees take up position all around the apartment. Grow roots. It will soon be Christmas. Growing up means putting down roots. She wonders how long and whether and how one can avoid growing up. Those who grow up, lose. 'Who are you then?'—'Yeahyeah.'—'Okay. Are you visiting, the owner or the tenant?'—'Yeahyeah.'—'Yeahyeah we'll soon see. Your identity card please, Yeahyeah.'—'This apartment makes a pleasant change from the other ones!'—'You can keep your compliments!'—'I'm not talking to you and I'm not paying compliments. That was meant for my colleagues.'

A hassle for the young policemen, carrying the red and white shelves from their library down the four flights of stairs. At every landing they stick out of the windows. Stolen goods, the building site boards. It was an effort to carry them up too. And what has happened to the books in the meantime?

It is cold. They are standing in the yard, huddled into one corner. Six months ago there were more of them, she thinks. She steps forward, just to try to get warm. A policeman barks at her, 'Stay where you are!'

Airfield, battle field, football field? Paths, ramps, stations, tracks, trains, going where?

The air battle over Berlin begins on 18 November 1943. On 22 November Potsdamer Platz goes up in flames. On 23 and 26 November blockbusters and bombs hit the ruined landscape once more.

You can count piles on Potsdamer Platz. Piles of sand, piles of rubble, mountains of stones, earth. Built up. The digger hums. A monotone, constant whine, pounding, but nothing is shaken. The piles grow bigger, turn into grown-up piles; they gradually grow towards each other and form banks, dams, dykes—if there were actually water on Potsdamer Platz you would think the noise of the diggers was the pitching of ships. But no river here, no dammed lakes. A dry spot, this building site, until they suddenly hit groundwater. The holes which go with the banks. Sometimes you think you can hear the sound of canons, gunfire. In the coming night the full moon will shine and stand clear over the area.

The old Weinhaus Huth upright and alone under the moonlight. An oasis, illuminated, inviting and a stronghold all at the same time, silent and proud. Recognizable from near and far by the small, eight-pillared tower on its roof. The whole building is a lighthouse, solitary in light-grey stone; with its oriels and high windows it emanates an old-fashioned glamour.

The delivery wagons for the party catering stand outside the house many days, to supply the receptions for the numerous men who sometimes wave; they all look quite similar, with their clothing, their haircuts, briefcases, their gaze and their gait. These men drive Mercedes, almost all of the cars have an S on the numberplate and are in dark colours. Later, at night, the security guards, who come back time and again, stop outside the door, the employees speak with a Saxony accent, and the police patrol in front of the last house left standing after the war.

What keeps her here still? The riots, the pallid romance of squatting? It was rarely comfortable in this house. Nothing more than a stronghold for border-crossers inside the walls of the city, made of stone. A small hot war, which they are losing, in the middle of the Cold War. The police dissolve the demonstration early, because the windows of a fur shop are smashed by missiles. Three demonstrators who try to hide in the entrance to a house are headed off by a police van. The first policeman to spring out beats one of the youths so hard that he nearly dies of four fractures to the skull.

It is getting more and more dangerous on the demonstrations; the more harmless the squatters have become over time, the fewer of them there are, the harder the police hit. Is that retaliation, what for? Cleaning up? She won't hold out much longer here either. Every stone ripped up will be thrown back, they say. She hasn't thrown a single stone. They are trespassing in a house that would have been demolished had it not been for them. One night the framework of the roof goes up in flames. The squatters put it out. One morning the cellar is under water, they bail it out. The house stays standing.

At night a cry in the yard.

'Agnes!' Almost a shriek. 'Agnes!' A window opens. A sleepy 'Yes?' Then very softly, 'Agnes, will you make tea?'—'What?' Obviously too quiet. Half one in the morning. 'Will you make a cup of tea?' Silence. 'I want to be with you.'—'What?'—'I want to be with you.'

Why can't you buy a pencil anywhere near the Kulturforum? No bread rolls, no tea, no shoes. Not a site for everyday things, rather a site for sensations. People on cords jump into the depths, individually for a few years, now in pairs. Children fly kites over the Führer's bunker. Fire-breathers at the medieval fair. The biggest circuses in the world pitch their tents. Pink Floyd and Elton John sing. Fireworks over the Reichstag on 3 October. Promises, gold fairs, laughing architecture. How to fill the new void, how to breathe life into the phantom of the two companies which own the heart of Berlin, peacefully cohabiting, which have occupied it with the help of a *coup d'état*, in the triangle of the Reichskanzlei,[4] the Gestapo headquarters and the Volksgerichthof?[5]

In a few years the moon will need to make a path through the narrow gorges of the music hall, department store, shopping mall and office buildings.

In between times, in between worlds appear. Hideouts, strange dwelling places, caves, nests, hiding places for those in need and in search of adventure. Bazaars, hawkers, cigarette sellers. The underworld comes up to the overworld. Above ground on the barren terrain and underground in the S-Bahn shafts. Still the barking of the dogs from the mobile home settlement, bordercrossers who live in old cars and caravans on the eastern side of the former Potsdam Station, where the Vaterland House used to stand, raising plants and children in between the wrecked cars, drums in the night.

Sometimes close to a hundred traders from the East, themselves border-crossers, who come over every Friday evening in tiny cars full of wares, which they also sleep in; a lively, animated babble of voices, palavering, haggling in

---

[4] Reich Chancellory.
[5] Nazi People's Court.

front of the Haus Huth, emptying vodka bottles, suddenly silence, running away when the police vans come, which chase them across the grass, herding them on ahead. A few moments later they are standing in groups back in their old positions. Babushka dolls, ten for twenty marks. After the Polish junk market had to vanish, the remaining groups on a Friday night are also driven away.

Mad runways after the time of complete traffic standstill at the former border-crossing, nowhere in the city is more open than here in the middle of the Wall, the margin has become the centre, chaos, tangled threads since the Wall opened, ever more streets but no routes. Hardly a taxi-driver knows how to get to the Weinhaus Huth; the address is free-floating, practically extra-terrestrial, at any rate hard to get to. Past the clinking *debis*-flags, there, where the Brothers Grimm lived, on the corner of Linkstraße recent black and white signs say 'Bannkreis'.[6] Opposite the Gropiusbau, in the Landtag, the former Prussian parliament building, the Berlin House of Representatives meet. Bannkreis. Under the ban of the sirens, but the police are only accompanying the latest state visit to the Brandenburg Gate with flashing lights and siren. The coaches rush past and the fuss dies down.

[6] Security zone around the Bundestag (parliament) where demonstrations are not allowed.

Photographers have climbed to the top of the Haus Huth, right to the tower. They are holding in their hands old photographs of the Platz when it was covered in buildings, trying to locate the Haus Vaterland, the Volksgerichthof, the Vox-Building, whereupon they photograph the emptiness, aiming confidently. The Weinhaus, where women were indulged, drank champagne in white furs and bodies decorated with rubies, ate caviar, is to become a real wine house again, even if the new buildings swallow up the tower.

They stood, thin dark punks, up on the roof at night and looked across the houses. They could see a long way, it was a clear night, the stars sparkled in their hair. They played the viola on the ridge of the roof. They had taken paint, painted hieroglyphs on the chimney pots. Nobody sleeps.

To Lichterfelde for work on the early S-Bahn. She sells things on a Turkish stall at the market, gets enough fruit and veg for nearly the entire house. In winter her feet stand in the snow until the tears come to her eyes. She buys herself moonboots, in which she feels like an elephant.

A dress of red, deep-red silk. And perhaps another time a white fur, and otherwise nothing but rubies on her body.

First bathe in milk and then drink champagne. Damned poverty. The money goes on coke, coke for the stove in the bathroom and coke for herself. They lie in bed freezing in the morning, they have no espresso and the cigarettes are finished. He heats the stove for hot water. How good their bodies smell! A mini bottle of bubbly is all there is in the fridge. The banana is too cold to eat. They try to warm it under the bedclothes. He dares to leave the bed for a moment, fetches two glasses for the Sekt. This winter they will only be able to get warm in bed. The stove heats the water hot, the minute it runs into the tub it goes cold again immediately. First bathe in milk, then drink champagne, then drape the white fur. 'Come on,' she says, 'you need to go. You can grin about her today.'

There is no exclamation mark on her Czech typewriter. A magical typewriter which suggests, then, with no exclamation mark, that she only write poetry, which means in fact, writing concrete poetry, which isn't so easy. She smiles. She would go to a funeral with this smile, walk into a nursery with utmost sincerity. I can take you anywhere, he says. When she first got to know him he consisted solely of opinions. They were all the more severe if he hadn't lived them. The pointless severity of youth. Clear-sighted and devoid of compassion, no creativity. He too would not be able to avoid growing up, she thinks now. You look like someone from the Weisse Rose[7] and I look like the Gestapo, he said a few days ago. Because he was wearing a leather coat? Two small boxes are lying in front of her, one box with coke, white, one box with his hair, black. Black and white, those aren't her colours any more. She sweeps both boxes from the table. The white powder mixes with the thin black lines on the floor.

Garish yellow and blue in the November *tristesse*, weighing down on Potsdamer Platz leaden and damp from the rain.

Between the blue and yellow containers and the blue and yellow site caravan, the workers; they wear blue and yellow hard-hats. Some of the containers which are stacked up in threes have curtains, behind which there are bed-frames, places to sleep for the workers who stay overnight on the building site. Babble of voices, scraps of Polish. There are no pubs, the nearest pizzeria some way away in Stresemannstraße, usually empty. New is a small white take-away stall at the edge of the traffic next to the remains of the Wall; a gate has formed from two segments of the Wall, turned around and intertwined, no-one goes through it.

The time of the Wall on Potsdamer Platz is over. Built-up excess pressure escapes. Construction fences are put up

[7] The White Rose, a group of resisters under the Nazis.

and block the view of the wide lawn. The grass where Curt
Bois stood and shouted, 'I can't find Potsdamer Platz.
Here—this can't be it!' In summer young couples used
to sun themselves between the rubble and the dandelions.
A gentleman dressed in white kneeled down in the open,
bent over till his forehead touched the ground, facing East,
facing Mecca. An older Turkish woman climbed the hazel
tree opposite the Philharmonic to gather nuts. The cars
with the prostitutes from Tiergartenstraße and their clients stopped in the cul-de-sac between Haus Huth and the
Staatsbibliothek, where a house once stood at Potsdamer
Straße 9, where Theodor Fontane used to live; they would
line up there in rows, the headlights went out, after a few
minutes they went on again, and the condoms were left
lying on the asphalt.

The lindens in front of Haus Huth are protected. They are
the only thing that still indicates the old route of
Potsdamer Straße, where the Staatsbibliothek was at
right angles. And the traces of the tram tracks which had
been covered with sand by the GDR border guards and
which have now been laid bare by the wind.

The lindens here blossom later than other lindens, and
they lose their leaves earlier.

A sky like lead, a sky which refuses to snow. Why won't it snow?

Sometimes she has to go out onto the street. She posts a letter, makes a phone-call. Two policemen in front of the house. On the other side of the street a drunk lies in the December slush. No-one pays any attention to him, not even the police. She eats standing up in the Turkish place. A drunk young man wants to hand in an empty beer bottle; the Turkish man won't take it. The German man discusses it for a while, but then has to retreat, not without remark. 'Think where you have got your riches from!' he yells. 'What riches?' she shouts after him. A full police van goes past her on Maaßenstraße. A coloured girl, a punk, stumbles into the gutter; three young people try to hail her a taxi, but the taxi-drivers shake their heads. The coloured girl yells deliriously, 'You twat, piss off!' She isn't drunk, she's wasted. At Nollendorfplatz a foreign girl holds a young woman's head. She throws up. An ambulance tears around Winterfeldtplatz.

More people than usual kill themselves at this time of year. Yet the rage on the street never comes. She goes back into the house which is nearly empty before Christmas. How many will come back, when will they be evicted, when will it be torn down?

Someone was killed. Run over by a bus, as he was chased by truncheons onto Potsdamer Straße after an eviction. The bus driver apparently hit the accelerator when the young man was already under the wheels. Hours later the police vans drive into the mourning crowd. The people sitting down jump up. The street cleaners follow the police van. They want to sweep up, the sand, the blood, the flowers. Yellow, white, green, orange—the colours of the public wagons. The orange wagon lowers its brushes. The traces will soon be removed. But then something unprecedented happens: No, you're not removing anything else here! Like wild animals five punks suddenly rush at the wagon, jump on the bumper as if they were barefoot, hammer on the windscreen with their fists, anger on their faces. They crouch, tiny figures, pale and bare and black, on the giant steel box. She watches in wonder as they force the street cleaning wagon to turn off. But the street is still swept, later.

That night the riots go on longer than usual. All the windows in the vicinity have been smashed. Her eyes are swollen from tear gas. At three in the morning she binds wounds and her own injured leg. They hear the first lies in the news, about the dead man and about his death. Three hours later she takes the S-Bahn to work in the market. All the windows are intact, the streets cleaned, no more stones, no shards, no barricades. But she feels the lemon in her pocket, which is supposed to help against tear gas, she is still wearing a black scarf round her neck. Her eyes are still swollen and red. So did she not dream it? As if it hadn't happened.

She's against the grand sweep of things; but on a small scale everything is becoming clearer.

In the evening the crows come, darken the sky behind the lindens, fly in formation over towards the Staatsbibliothek. A sky which refuses to snow.

Remains of the Esplanade

Annett Gröschner

The way she walked, who could describe it?

With her arms spread out wide, balancing, as if she had a beam beneath her feet, and below that a certain drop, dangerous for her bones, one false step and she would miss her footing, come off the path. Path? At first glance there's no path here and at second glance a few footpaths off to the horizon. Calling this a square was a mistake. City, who had said city here? Here was neither *urbs* nor *civitas*. Just emptiness. These marks which she measured in paces were described by older generations of chroniclers as the heart of the city. The chroniclers were dead, and the last storyteller desperately searched for Café Josty, which he thought he had seen in another time, a time which had been his. Death had forgotten him. The city, a juridical person in the files of the highest financial authorities, had cut its own heart out in sheer thoughtlessness, and then neatly divided the hole into two halves. So the city lay there now, heartless.

Her old rule of not stepping in the cracks between the paving stones didn't apply. There were none, only the kerbstones which separated the pavement from the street. The pavements were mud, and the houses. Where were the houses? Castles in the air with invisible windows, reflecting a grey sky. Hypothetical birds nesting on the balconies. And she didn't know any more whether she was behind the windows or in front of them, was she in this time or another or caught in an imagination which had displaced reality fifty years ago? What was she looking for here? A cobblestone which she prised from the sand with the tip of her foot?

The big city is built entirely on sand / you let it run through your fingers senselessly / and impatiently / for clear sight and the burden of knowing / that everything falls and set right again / falls again / gives strange movement to thought / and big words are written in sand
she whispers, her arms still spread out wide. The woman who had written that was no longer here either.[1]

---

[1] The poet, Inge Müller.

She tried to encompass the square with her arms. Her right hand described the street to the Brandenburg Gate, Königgrätzer Straße, Friedrich-Ebert-Straße, Hermann-Göring-Straße, the Wall, Friedrich-Ebert-Straße, as many names as the city had governments. The time before last it had been reduced to a patrol route for the plastic bucket cars which kept the left chamber of the heart from the right, or vice versa, depending on which direction you had approached the square from. Her left arm described another wasteland, which had once been a station, from where the trains departed for Paris. Rails descending upon rails where lines converged on each other only to diverge again. Each went its separate way simply lying there on the ground before disappearing completely. There was no exit to the world here. Coming from Leipziger Straße, past the decaying entrances to the underground, she had walked round the octagon of the square in front of them, a square which could no longer be distinguished from the other, more important one. There was another story underneath this site, inaccessible and secret, a story of drowning, people clinging to the rails which knew a way out but wouldn't divulge it. She could no longer find the gates of the Excise Wall[2] on the map from 1936 in the real world.

---

[2] The old city wall.

In the Lenné Triangle[3] weeds ran riot, as if they were authorized to do so, right in the middle of the city. They came up at the corner above the foundations of the Columbus House, with its neon adverts, with its burnt-out upper floors, out of place on the square, which had turned into the world and then turned into wasteland in layers, which was also unfair. For the border guards, who had strewn poison around the area so that the plants didn't obscure their sightlines, were no longer there either. The kerbstone of chunky granite had outlasted them. Who noticed kerbstones. They could stay unseen, they could last. Four feet to the next crack, four feet to the next foot.

Who did this foot belong to, in the brown clumpy shoe, thirties-style? It belonged to a standing leg, standing between two feet of a tripod, which were blocking her way.

Get out of my picture, the figure said, its head covered with a cloth which ended in a lens.

Get out of my story, the woman said and peered down the glass of the lens.

Shit, the lens swore, *now you've spoiled my picture.*

---

[3] A small area of land which belonged to the GDR, but was on the West side of the Wall; squatters took up residence here with impunity until the West Berlin police stormed it in July 1988, whereupon the squatters escaped to the East.

—*A picture of what?*

—*A picture of emptiness. Archaeologists say that when you get to the very bottom of a site, what is left is emptiness.*

—*But before the emptiness is left, the traces must have been excavated. Have you got them on your photos too? Have you seen the number twenty-five tram line?*

—*The tracks are under the asphalt,* said the man, who had removed his cloth.

—*And can you see the conductors too?* asked the woman.

—*I'm not interested in the conductors, I'm interested in the interiors they moved in. You have to hold on to the traces before they disappear again, before they are sealed in concrete. They think their constructions are for all eternity, and eternity is nothing more than their lifetime, when they are dead everything turns to dust, but they aren't interested in that. There are moments when the traces lie bare. A fleeting moment of sensibility, where the ages are visible in layers. You stare and stare and can't get enough of it. You stay hungry to hold on to this moment. And then it happens that you hold on too long and can't find your place in time any more.*

—*I know,* she said, *but I'm interested in the stories behind the traces. This square is like the empty gaze of someone suffering from memory loss. I want the memory.*

—*My spot is in front of the gate. You get the best view of the city there. And the loneliest.*

—My spot is on the marketplace in front of the gate, where the stories come together. But you're still lonely amidst the babble of voices too.

It was ten o'clock on the twenty-sixth of February. The way across the carriageway on Bellevuestraße with a backwards glance at the edges of the city behind the Potsdam Gate led to the vestiges of a house which had survived as a ruin. The remains of the Esplanade.

They walked into the hotel reception. The cloakroom attendant took the heavy case from the photographer and said, *We don't actually take luggage.*

—*We're only here for a coffee,* said the man.

—*That's what lots of people have said and they've never come back,* murmured the old woman, her sight wasn't as clouded as the mirrors on the walls. She took the case anyway.

FOLLOW THE RED CARPET FOR THE BAR.

They followed it obediently and without speaking. Up a flight of stairs into the Red Room. A room with outdated glamour lay before them, with marble pillars on the pink painted walls, golden stucco work everywhere, curved mirrors reaching to the high red ceiling, a Belle Epoque fireplace. The parquet creaked.

This room you are in is the Kaiser's room, which is so called because Wilhelm II celebrated gentlemen's evenings here, said the woman.

—*Were you there?* asked the man.

—*As I said, they were gentlemen's evenings.*

The restaurant had shut.

They walked ten metres further to the breakfast room, reached by going down a broad staircase. Neo-rococo on the yellowing walls, mirror, fireplace, and an arched lattice window reaching from the floor to the ceiling. Some of the mirrors had been shattered in one of the last bombing raids and had been replaced by frosted glass. They walked past them and expected to see an image, but the glass didn't reflect anything.

—*This was the place for demi-mondaines, speculators and the elegant bourgeoisie*, the woman said.

—*Were there photographers?* asked the man.

—*There have always been gigolos with cameras here and everywhere. They used to dance the tango in the evening with the demi-mondaines and invite them to visit their workshops.*

—*Did the ladies accept?*

—*It depended how cleverly they put it.*

The waitress gave off an air of *fin-de-siècle* charm in her lack of haste in coming to the table and the slow way she looked the photographer up and down. The woman watched it not without satisfaction. Why should it only be photographers who eye people up? With her left foot the waitress removed her right shoe and slipped it back on. The ball of her foot was pretty. She didn't have any bread rolls.

—*Delivery is really bad at the moment.*

She didn't go straight to the kitchen with their order, instead she went over to another table and said to an older gentleman:

—*Give me your phone number sir, we might never see each other again.*

—*I don't have my phone number in my head.*

—*What do you imagine it would have been like if we had met in the forties?* asked the photographer.

—*We wouldn't have called each other by our first names.*

—*I beg your pardon madam.*

—*I would have met you while you were taking photographs, you would have been using the same camera, wearing the same shoes.*

—*What would I have been photographing?*

—*At this point in time sir, 1945, you are taking photographs of the destruction on the North–South Axis, under commission from Speer's office, who are secretly pleased, the bombardments have of course cleared space for the capital Germania. You are a freelance photographer, have only been spared the front because you have a liver complaint. You are actually a little yellower in the face, and sometimes you are subject to comments because of your supposedly Jewish appearance.*

—And you?

—At the time when we meet, my husband is on the Oder front, I don't love him, secretly hope sometimes that he won't come back. I am having a liaison with an artist who has got out of being sent to the front because of alleged mental incapacity, I visit his partially destroyed studio after breakfast on coupons. He is a good lover. My children have been evacuated to the country. I want to send for them before the war comes to the streets of Berlin. Today I was ordered to go and build barricades in Hochmeisterstraße. I didn't go, because everything seems pointless to me.

Suddenly the sirens wail, the light goes out. The waitress comes over to the table.

—I'll take you to the air raid shelter.

They go through the lobby, down another set of stairs, past the bathrooms with marble toilets and urinals.

The cellar is dark and stuffy, phosphorus markings indicate the way to the shelter. There are not many guests left on this twenty-sixth of February, 1945. They are hard to make out in the darkness. They see the waitress and the elderly gentleman in a corner of the room. They sit down next to a wall. They can hear the motors of the airplanes.

They can hear the dull thunder of the guns and the bombs exploding. They get closer and closer. It is deathly quiet in the room. They hear the bombers droning over the hotel. The carpet bombing seems as if it will never end. A whistling sound...they all brace themselves in anticipation of collapse. A crash, a thud, shaking, the cellar lifts up and drops back down into the foundations. Lime dust covers everything, the ceiling has a wide crack.

Suddenly it is quiet. No-one knows any more how much time has passed. She looks at her watch. It is 12.05. When someone opens the door smoke comes in from outside. The woman holds a cloth in front of her face.

—*The whole of Potsdamer Platz is burning, so is the back of the hotel. Try the emergency exits!*

They go up and down stairs in the thick smoke. The fire shatters the window panes in the Kaiser's room. He drags her down the stairs into the vestibule. The cloakroom attendant is standing at the counter:

—*I didn't think you would come back. Here is your case. I sat on it during the raid, if you don't mind.*

As they leave the Esplanade the open square is lying in the sun.

—*I don't like the sun, it spoils my pictures*, the photographer grumbles and puts his camera down by the exit.

Hopefully it will go behind the clouds. The invisible birds fly over the invisible Columbus House.

—*Say hello to your lover,* says the photographer.

—*Stories come to life through the inventions which give them truthfulness.*

—*Get out of the picture then, I need it to be empty of people.*

The way she walks, with arms spread out wide, balancing, as if she had a beam beneath her feet, and below that a certain drop, dangerous for her bones, who could describe it?

And why?

For a Handful of Loose Change

Carmen Francesca Banciu

Friday in the U-Bahn.

I like travelling. I like travelling on the U-Bahn. From Mitte to Charlottenburg. And back. From Mitte to Kreuzberg. Or somewhere else. And always back to Mitte. My Mitte, my centre. And the centre of Berlin.

It was on a Friday evening. And I had to go travelling again. I didn't feel like doing anything but still had to go out into town. Felt like I had been tricked.

Unenthusiastically I got into the U-Bahn. The last few weeks hung from my shoulders like buckets full of water that wobbled and sloshed over the sides with every step and trickled into my shoes. The feeling disgusted me. And with every step I thought I was trampling to bits shreds of the past which were peeling off like dead skin in my wet shoes. I slid around in my suddenly too big shoes, and tried to make progress. The wet things tried to stop me. I got in the train and sat down at the window. Looked at my figure which was reflected in it and asked myself what I must look like with this burden that threatened to buckle me. In the mirror you couldn't see anything. You couldn't see to look at me the fears that I took out walking, and I was amazed at my huge ability to repress things. I had been carrying this burden around with me for years. Some weeks ago it had become unbearable. Sometimes I went travelling to try to discard a bit of it. To leave the fear behind in a train somewhere. And to get out again so quickly it was threatening to suffocate me. I couldn't imagine I would ever be separated from it. What I wanted to do most was stay at home. In bed. So that the weight was spread and my shoulders didn't have to buckle. I felt I was at the mercy of this weight and in danger of getting caught in its spell. And I am a happy person. I know that unhappiness is a difficult addiction.

I sat in the train and thought about addiction. It was a word that had occupied me for weeks. It wasn't my addiction. It was addiction to the addictions of other people. I am a happy person. I know all that. I just can't always resist the addiction to the addictions of others. Sitting next to me was a small melancholic man. He could have been in his prime. A bedraggled tomcat looking for the nearest shelter. Opposite him a young couple with ideals and sparkle in their eyes. They were deep in conversation. The bedraggled cat could have been in his prime. If the traces of his past hadn't oppressed him so much. There was something childlike and sad about him. As if he had had to stop playing games much too young. And as if he had never got over it. He watched the couple for a while. Then he said, I presume you have no idea who Mick Jagger is. A great man. You, he said. And looked the boy in the eye. You probably weren't even a twinkle. When he was famous. Then he produced a harmonica from his pocket and began to play. He was small and delicate. His old blue jeans, his trembling hands, the melancholy. His hair so uncombed. A neglected lawn. The music trembled and flowed into the space. The little man wiped his arm across his moustache and carried on playing. A beer can was standing at his feet. After the song he took a large gulp. So large he had to tip his head far back. He played another song. A sad one. Then he looked at the man opposite in his unencumbered youth and asked: Got any spare change?

You want some change. The youth seemed to wake up suddenly. He searched through his pockets and gave him all the change he could find. The man smiled shyly and showed his toothless mouth. Was pleased with his bounty. I wondered if I should also give him some change. But he didn't want anything from me. He looked at the other people in the train, but they ignored him. We came into Potsdamer Platz. A bundle of energy with a guitar stormed into the carriage. His voice woke all the passengers. He sang about love and life and politics. About taxes, war, and ecology. About politicians, Eichel, Fischer, and the Berlin Republic. A troubadour for the metropolis and democracy. Every head turned towards him. Suddenly life was flowing. And my addiction to addiction drained away. People were clamouring to fill the troubadour's cap and left the carriage happy. The bedraggled cat pulled out his harmonica and accompanied the bundle of energy in a minor key, to emphasize life's ambivalence. I too handed my obol to the singer with great joy and got out at Bismarckstraße. In my exuberant mood I tore the clip-on earring from my ear. A silver ball, which fell onto the platform and rolled onto the tracks in front of the conductor's office. A man came out of the office and said: Now I'll show you what the BVG[1] can do. He climbed down onto the tracks and fetched the earring for me. Wiped it clean on his uniform. And handed the piece of jewellery back to me with a triumphant gesture.

---

[1] Berliner Verkehrsgesellschaft, now Verkehrsbetriebe, the transport company that runs the Berlin underground.

As I left the underground station my shoulders felt pleasant. My mood had changed. People wouldn't believe what kind of miracles happen on short journeys. And all that for a handful of loose change.

Something for Nothing

Larissa Boehning

In early autumn, the swallows leave the North. They criss-cross the sky in wide sweeping ribbons, drop away, dart side to side in the air, soar up again effortlessly, full of strength for the flight south. They only come back in the spring, fix their nests under the roof and live in these cracks during the year. You could follow the swallows' path along the dyke when they went south. They always flew over the land, never over the sea. When they went, you knew that autumn was coming. They take the light with them, some-one once said. When they are gone, it gets dark.

He sold me his orangey-red Swallow moped. He said, 'One swallow doesn't make a summer,' laughed as he said it. His face was broad, his beard stubbly and dense. He was wearing a dark blue cap. He introduced himself as Uli Fähnlein—'Little Flag'—'and I am the kind of person who's blowing in the wind, or something,' he laughed again. I thought, what a strange person with his sad laugh.

We went for a test drive through Neukölln, stopped by the bank, I took out 400DM. In front of his shop I counted it into his hand. It was windy, he laid his hand on mine and we ended up shaking hands.

'And if you need a camera,' he said, pointing to his shop window, 'always come to me.' 'Why?' I asked, one foot on the starter, hands on the handlebars. 'I'll tell you that if you actually show up.'

On the day it happened I wheeled the Swallow out of the house and was just driving up the street, past the photo shop, when Uli called to me. I stopped, and he checked whether all the lights were working. 'It's not bad,' he said, 'it does sixty.' I nodded and drove off in the direction of the city centre.

The phone-call came in the early evening, I'd just come home. My mother couldn't stop crying, I couldn't ask her what had happened. I got on a train and went north. I arrived around midnight, a grey car was still standing in front of the house. 'They've already come for him,' my mother said as I came into the hallway, 'they just took him away.'

I didn't see my father again, just saw how he had left everything. His workbench in his hobby room, the tweezers and the soldering iron lay around as if they had only just been put down, as if he would come back any moment and tidy everything away.

I stayed until the funeral. The morning after, my mother said, 'Take the cameras away with you, I don't want the things here any more, they all stare at me.' I took them away with me, pulled the heavy bag across the station. My mother raised her hand and waved goodbye, I just asked her if she would cope with everything.

I put the bag with the cameras out in the hall, I didn't want them standing in my room. The next morning I carried them over the road to the photo shop. Uli was sitting on a folding stool in front of the shop window, drinking coffee. 'Ah, well, well,' he said, 'want something to drink?' He watched as I put the bag down and sat down next to him. 'What's happened here?' he asked, his gaze searched my face, he turned round to look at me. I told him about my father. 'Killed by smoking,' Uli said quietly, and shook his head, 'I'm sorry.' I sat there next to him, our arms were touching. I opened the bag and said, 'Have a look.' He took them out one by one, turned over the cases, pressed the shutter release over and again, there was a metallic click in the cameras' insides. 'They're good,' Uli said appreciatively, 'did he collect them?' 'Yes,' I replied, 'haven't seen him take photos for years, he just put the things in the cabinet and took them out every now and then to clean them or to fiddle around with them.'

'I can't give you any money for them,' Uli said, 'I'll have to sell some of them first.' I nodded. I didn't want to carry the bag any more and didn't want the lenses' empty eyes in my flat. 'Will you get rid of them?' I asked, and was immediately ashamed of the question. 'The Nikons are on a run just now,' Uli said, business-like, 'the Voigtländers are probably too old, no-one's buying that kind of thing just now, but all the Olympus stuff will go, I'm sure about that.'

He offered me some coffee, I shook my head. 'Don't you want to keep any of them?' he asked. A car revved loudly outside. 'I'll think about it,' I said, although I was sure I didn't want to have any of the cameras.

He looked at me for a moment. We were still sitting close to each other. I saw the large pores in the skin on his nose, his face. He had a very particular smell about him, part early-morning sleepiness, part cigarettes, and something old, maybe from the dust that was also lying around in the shop. He stood up, pushed the bag behind the counter, locked the door, hung a sign on it—'SHORT BREAK!'—and sat down next to me again.

'Shall we go for a little walk?' he asked and pushed his cap back and forwards with a swift movement. I nodded.

'Let's take the Swallow,' he said, 'then we can go further out.'

We went into my yard, I picked up my helmet. 'The boss will drive today,' Uli said, levered the Swallow off its stand and pushed it out of the yard. I got on behind him and held on around his waist. He was fat, his belly was firm. It was odd being so close to him. He was wearing a bobbly knitted jumper and a red scarf around his neck. He looked like a captain who no longer had a ship. He said, 'I'll show you something beautiful, kid.' As we started off I pressed myself closer to him. If anyone had asked, I would have said it was good, sitting behind him like that. Although I barely knew him. He just seemed like a friend, a confidant who'd just happened to come along.

We drove from Neukölln towards Kreuzberg, along the Landwehrkanal, drove once through Treptow Park. I signalled to him from behind, 'Keep going straight ahead,' he shook his head under the helmet. We parked at the foot of the Schlesische Brücke in front of an old petrol station. It was quiet, by comparison: I had got used to the loud noise of the engine. He pulled his helmet off his head, I carried on wearing mine. We walked over some factory grounds, through a rusty door and stood in an abandoned hall.

'Here's where we always used to practise,' he said.

'Practise what?' I asked.

'With our band,' Uli laughed, 'I'll show you the photos.'

'When?' I asked him, we went further into the hall, there was something in front of us not dissimilar to a steam locomotive. Next to it a puddle of rusty water. The smooth surface reflected the blind windows, the steel girders on the ceiling.

'Beginning of the Nineties,' Uli said, 'just after the Wall came down, everything here has been abandoned since then.' We crossed the hall, water was dripping somewhere. Uli took my arm, 'Come on, I'll show you something completely way-out.' We climbed up to the first floor via a narrow ladder. For a short moment I was surprised that I was following him just like that.

We came into a room with steel lockers, the doors open and dented. A shoe was lying in one locker, as if someone might come and pick it up some time.

'It gets better,' Uli said. We walked past a washroom, the sinks stood in the middle like troughs, the mirrors on the wall rusted away in patches. On a ledge lay a dirty chunk of soap.

'Someone's been here recently,' I said, and looked at Uli. He laughed. 'We'll soon see,' he whispered, 'come on.' I shoved my hands in my trouser pockets. I was still wearing my helmet. Uli pulled open an iron door. We came into a large room with rows of broad workbenches. Lying on top was a jumble of tools, metal, engine parts. It looked as if the workers had left everything standing or lying there when a bell sounded, home time, off, gone. I was silent. Uli reached for an oil-smeared hammer. 'That's a good tool,' he said, 'look here.' We walked between the rows of benches, Uli pocketed some tongs and a few screwdrivers. The air in the room was heavy, metallic, and dusty.

'That's how a state comes to an end,' he said as he walked, 'deserted by everyone. Could have happened to us too, it happens so fast—you can see here just how fast it happens.' I nodded. Uli carried on walking through the rows. 'It's a nice image: the people simply leave everything behind, leave it all lying, in the factories, on the assembly lines, they don't go in the shops, there's no-one sitting at the tills, the buses and trains stay in the depots in the morning. I like that image,' he said quietly.

'What would you do,' I asked him, 'on a day like that?' He laughed. It was that serious laugh again, from someone who wears his despair just under the surface of his skin. 'I'd just sit in front of the shop, and watch the people in the street running from shop to shop, all of them shut or empty, no-one serving, and I'd watch them standing there not knowing what to do or where to go.' I grinned, took my helmet off, held it like a shopping basket and collected some work tools. 'So then you'd go shopping', I shouted to him from one of the back rows, 'until there was nothing left.' 'And then,' Uli shouted back, 'we'd drive out to the allotments, go to mum's, she's always got some potatoes spare.'

'Is there stuff here I could use for my moped?' I looked at him.

Uli had come over to me. He was gathering some smaller screwdrivers, shoving the tools to and fro on the bench with his fleshy hands.

'Take what you need,' I said. 'Yes, boss,' he laughed, 'that's called plundering a state.' 'What do you mean, a state,' I said, 'everything's just lying around here.'

'Maybe it's like a museum,' he grinned, 'do you take things from museums too?'

'That's different,' I said quickly. He had come right up to me, looked me right in the face.

'Sometimes you really like being a girl.'

'I don't have any other choice.' I turned away.

He moved off, propped himself against the doorframe with one hand. 'Our expedition carries on,' he said quietly, and turned to go. I cast another glance over the work-benches, I had the strange impression that the sounds of the work, the machines, still hung in the room. Uli called to me. I went to the workbench and grabbed a wrench. I moved the cold metal to and fro across the table. There were stubbed-out cigarette butts everywhere in the gaps. My father often used to rest his cigarette on the edge of the work-surface when he needed two hands. The smoke curled up in the air, the ash fell down to the ground. My mother had always swept the workroom in the evening, conscientiously removing the remains of his work. I heard Uli calling to me again. I went into the stairwell, he was standing halfway up. 'Come on,' he said emphatically.

We walked through a corridor and came onto an open balcony with a brick balustrade. In front of us was a waterway leading into the Spree.

'The border was here, over there was the West.' He pointed out the huge searchlights which were fixed to the roofs of the houses nearby. 'Was once a well-guarded crossing.'

I leaned over the balustrade, saw the dark water of the canal. Rubbish and planks of wood were swimming along the narrow banks.

'It was all full of barbed wire round here until just recently,' he said slowly, 'someone or other started to remove it. Safety reasons, probably,' he added, and laughed. 'They used to patrol up and down along this balcony.'

'Did anyone ever make it?' I asked, my belly still pressed up against the balustrade.

'I think so,' said Uli, 'I heard once that a man tried to swim across here.' He pushed himself off from the balustrade, wandered down the corridor. On the bank opposite I could see an allotment site, with squat sheds, brightly coloured umbrellas, a jetty where small boats were tied up.

'Looks like a peaceful life over there,' I said as Uli came back and stood next to me.

'But not exactly my dream destination either,' he said.

'If you could just go away somewhere, where would you go?' I asked him suddenly. He picked up his helmet.

'Greece, one of the islands,' he said quickly, 'I went there once to a small house in the mountains. From the top you had a clear view of the sea.'

'Why don't you do it?' I asked. He reached for a screw which was lying on the balustrade and threw it far into the Spree. 'Let's go. I want to show you something else.'

Carrying our helmets like baskets, we went down the fire-escape stairs to the floor below. We were back in the corridor which seemed to run along the building on the side nearest the Spree. Through the bars of the railing I could see the other river bank. It smelled of urine and stagnant water. 'I'd like to introduce you to someone,' Uli said, and went on ahead.

At the end of the corridor a steel door stood ajar. Uli disappeared, I followed him. It led into a high, square room, canvases, stone sculptures and figures made of bits of iron welded together everywhere. Uli shouted, 'Come here, kid.' I was annoyed that he was calling me that here.

'Wolfgang, what's up?' Uli asked in a loud voice. 'Hey,' said Wolfgang, and carried on rolling his cigarette. His greasy hat had slipped down his neck. His face was grey as dust. He screwed his eyes up and looked at me. His eyebrows were broad, a few hairs stood out like spiders' legs. Uli was talking as if he had to talk for three. Wolfgang lit the crumpled cigarette behind a cupped hand, the room smelled of petrol and dust. I looked around and put my helmet down, even though I wanted to go. 'Uli,' I began. 'What are you after here?' interrupted Wolfgang and looked at Uli. 'Just wanted to see if you're still alive,' he answered. 'Thanks for that,' said Wolfgang. Uli looked uncertain, looked around, looked at me. A door banged and a woman came from the back of the room. Her long dark blond hair hung down her like two stripes. 'That's Inge,' Uli said to me.

'I'm Inge,' the woman repeated, once she was standing next to me. She was very thin, and had no bust whatsoever. Wolfgang was smoking, Uli swung his helmet and let it knock against his legs. The tools inside knocked against each other and made metallic noises.

'Did you get those upstairs?' Inge asked.

'Yes,' I said quickly, and saw that she was scrutinizing my helmet. 'So you've gone and taken the best bits,' Inge said. Her voice was sharp and strangely hollow.

'Okay you two,' Uli said, 'we've got to head off.' I nodded to Inge. 'Yeah, hey,' Wolfgang called after us.

Outside Uli caught my gaze. 'He's lost his sense of humour,' he said. It was more a question. I said, 'No wonder, with a girlfriend like that.' Uli laughed briefly. 'Come on, kid, let's get back.' For a brief second I wondered why he kept calling me that.

He stopped the Swallow in front of the shop, put the stand down. I stood on the pavement, the pockets in my jacket hung low with the tools in. 'What are you up to tonight?' he asked, trying to be casual. I took everything out of my pockets, saw that my hands were smeared with dirt and said, 'I've got plans already.' He unlocked the door, took the tools out of my hands and went inside. 'Are they staying here?' I asked. He said, 'If the Swallow breaks down it'll be me who repairs it anyway.' 'Okay,' I drawled, 'I'll remind you of that when the time comes.' Uli had disappeared into the cellar. I stood there, uncertain. Everywhere I looked there was stuff, cameras, cine-cameras, magazines, old leather photo bags. The wall behind the sales counter was covered in photos. I recognized Uli on them. One picture showed five lads in green light, a band, the singer was jumping up with his legs wide, leaning on the mike stand. In the background a man was hanging on a rope from the ceiling like a cocoon, upside down. I heard Uli coming up the steps. 'Was that you?' I asked. Uli's gaze followed where my finger was pointing. 'Yes, that was us. I'm the one at the back.'

'What,' I laughed, 'the one hanging?'

'No, that's not me,' said Uli, 'that's Wolfgang, I'm the one here.' He pointed to the jumping singer. 'We used to do the music for his happenings. Was a fun time.' He went out the back again, I heard a cassette recorder clattering as a tape was put in. The music filled the shop. Uli stood in the hallway, looked at me and grinned.

I drove the Swallow into town to work, but not up our street, not past the photo shop. On Saturday morning I found a note in my letterbox saying 'You haven't exactly won the lottery, but I've sold two Nikons. Come over, Uli.'

I went to the photo shop, sat myself down on the folding stool which stood outside, and waited until Uli finished serving all the customers. 'Alright, kid,' he greeted me. I was glad that he didn't seem to mean anything by it. We drank some coffee. In the pub across the street a woman had a go at a man. A girl walked past, pulling her dog behind her, right in front of us he pissed against a tree.

'And, what have you been up to?' Uli asked. I wondered what I ought to tell him. He stood up suddenly, went into the shop. I thought, does he want to hear or not. 'Sorry,' he said, when he came back out again, 'you can start now.' I said nothing.

From across the street a little man came towards us. 'Fähnlein,' the figure shouted and grinned, 'leave the women alone.' 'I haven't done anything,' shouted Uli, holding up his hands. 'That's Hoffmann,' he said to me, and when Hoffmann was standing in front of him, 'Hi, how's it going today?'

'It's going,' said Hoffmann, 'it's going.' He was wearing a greasy suit which had got too big for him, the trousers were held together by a belt with a buckle. 'Got anything for me?' Hoffmann asked, 'I might have some spare capacity': he pronounced *capacity* slowly and clearly, as if he had just learnt the word and wanted to try out how it sounded.

'Yeah, I've got some stuff lying around here,' Uli said, went into the shop and returned with two old cameras. 'These belong to the lady here,' Uli said. 'This one has something wrong with the shutter release. And on this one the catch sticks sometimes.'

'Fine, fine,' said Hoffmann, 'that can be sorted.'

As he went, I said to Uli, 'I can't believe they're broken, my father would definitely have repaired them.'

'They aren't broken,' said Uli and raised his coffee cup. 'But Hoffmann needs something to do. Otherwise he'll just think about the fact that it will all be over soon.' I was silent.

'You work and work and then you fall off your stool,' Uli said and laughed his sad laugh, 'what else is there?'

'Hm, whatever comes in between,' I said.

A customer went into the shop, Uli followed, and I stayed where I was. When he came out again, he said, 'I'm taking photos at a kind of art thing this evening. One of Wolfgang's. If you fancy it, you could come along too.'

We drove there on the Swallow. Uli didn't talk much, I was quiet too, there was something cold about him. I couldn't have said what. I followed him across the car park. The light from a couple of street lamps was reflected in the expanse of puddle surfaces. It was part of the factory grounds that we'd been in a while ago. We climbed down a narrow ladder and stood with our heads tucked in under the arches of the ceiling. Uli nodded to me. I lost myself among the crowd. The room slowly filled up, we stood under the low ceiling and breathed in the smell of the damp plasterwork.

Inge came over to me. 'I know you,' she said, 'you're Uli's girlfriend aren't you?' I shook my head, was going to say that I wasn't his girlfriend, just a friend, and said yes.

She came and stood right up close to me. I moved away a bit.

'He's a good bloke,' Inge said loudly, 'I can see that. Just a bit fat.' I thought of dusty Wolfgang, his sinuous, almost gouty hands, which had lit the cigarette and said, 'I don't think so.'

'Nah, course not,' Inge said, 'love makes you blind. I'm like that too.'

I said nothing.

'Do you know Uli married a friend of mine?' Inge looked at me searchingly.

'No, I didn't know,' I said, and tried to look uninterested.

'Yeah well, it's a while ago now,' she said, 'and it really was an emergency.'

I couldn't help it, and looked questioningly at her.

'Was before the Wall came down,' she remarked. On the stage in front a lump of meat slapped to the floor. Blood spurted. 'A friend of mine, she was pregnant and wanted to leave for the West. So he married her. She claimed that the child was his.'

'And was it?' I asked.

'No idea. You don't know what goes on in other people's beds,' Inge said, and looked at me. Her lips were narrow, and her make-up went over the edges. She was wearing a smock with deep cut-out armholes and no bra underneath. At the front something slapped again, a floppy, wet sound.

'You can ask him about it,' she said, 'but I don't think he likes talking about it.'

It struck me that Uli wore a broad gold ring, which almost seemed to have grown into his finger, I had noticed it the very first time we met, when I had bought the Swallow. It looked antique. I had thought then that he was wearing his parents' old wedding ring.

'He looked after her well,' Inge said. 'That's what my friend always said.' She said it with a tone of appreciation, but also complicity: I know more than you, I know other things that you don't know about, and if you ask me I might tell you. But I didn't fancy asking her, I said, 'I need to go get something to drink.'

I found Uli at the back of the room. He was leaning against a wall, one leg bent, and was putting a film in the camera. 'Kid,' he said, 'is this your kind of thing?' He put his hand on my arm and said, 'Have you seen, Inge is here, that's someone you know already, even if she's not some-one you like talking to.'

'It's okay,' I said, 'we've already said hello.'

'Ah,' said Uli, and looked at me. 'Wolfgang with his meat, it's mad, isn't it?'

I nodded and drank.

'But I've taken a couple of fun photos, some real slabs with loads of blood.'

'It smells really strong in here,' I said quietly, as Uli turned away. He went back to the stage, I stood where I was, and looked at the backs of the people in front of me. I had wanted to ask him if it had really been like that.

Later, as he came over to me, he asked, 'Do you want to stay or go?' His voice was deep, heavy with beer, the camera lens pressed against my hip as he leant towards me.

'I want to go,' I said quickly, 'but I don't want to go home.'

'Enough meat for today,' Uli said and led the way up the small ladder.

The night was lukewarm, a clear sky and no wind. We sat down on the edge of the kerb, stretched out our legs and both looked straight ahead.

'That was it, once,' Uli said then, 'but it's over. You can't get it back.'

I thought of Inge, her boney breast, her over-lipsticked mouth, which opened and shut silently. In a strange way I'd got a bit of a fright when he said it was over. He was silent, I asked, 'What?' and looked at him from the side.

'The time when I used to think that was good. That something like that was good.'

'Dropping meat?'

'Yes, everything, the whole fuss and nonsense. It isn't what matters. None of it is what actually matters.'

Two women walked past us across the car park and laughed loudly. I lay down on my back on the pavement, Uli scrutinized me from above. I folded my hands across my stomach.

'You're lying in the dirt, kid,' Uli said slowly. 'Doesn't matter,' I said.

'Doesn't matter, nothing matters,' Uli said and laughed scornfully. 'I'd love to run through the city at night, screaming, nothing matters! Wake everyone up out of their dreams and scream, do you hear me, you idiots, nothing matters!'

'I'm with you,' I said. He looked at me, astonished. I sat up, rubbed my hands and said it again, 'Come on, let's go.'

We got onto the Swallow, raced over the cobblestones back to Neukölln and screamed above the sound of the engine for the whole journey. We drove through the night, the smell of the two-stroke in our noses, and I held on tight to Uli's waist, leaned back and screamed. Uli leaned forwards, into the headwind, and screamed louder than me. We were an Ascension Day commando. We were drunk.

It was a while before we saw each other again. My Swallow wouldn't start and I wheeled it out of the yard, across the street over to the photo shop. Uli wasn't there, the sign was hanging on the door and I thought, then I'll wait.

He came round the corner, out of Sonnenallee. He was holding an ice-cream in front of him, a few scoops in a tub. When he was standing in front of me, he pulled the light blue paper umbrella out of the ice-cream and threw it on the road.

'I've always loved those,' I said. He bent down slowly and picked it up. 'Here,' he said, 'it's for you. If I'd known you were going to show up, I'd have brought you an ice-cream.'

I unfurled the umbrella, ran my finger carefully over the paper, thin as silk, and twirled it between my thumb and forefinger.

'Something up with the Swallow?' he said, as he walked into the shop. I followed him.

'It won't start.'

He repeated the sentence, drawing out the words, turned round to face me and said, 'Well I guess Uli Fähnlein will have to repair it then.'

I didn't say anything, just looked at him. I was about to say, you're the one with the tools, but kept quiet instead. He went behind the counter, tidied some money away into the till, sorted out some receipts, then said suddenly, 'The girl only comes when she wants something. And when you aren't expecting her any more.'

I shoved my hands in my trouser pockets and stood in the door with my stomach sticking out. 'You said you would repair it.' Uli looked at me for a moment. 'But not today,' he said, 'today I need some peace and quiet for once.'

I tried to smile, he walked past me.

'I'm going back down the cellar,' he said, 'I can get some peace there.'

He bent down under the counter, rummaged in a chest. He seemed to be looking for something.

'Another time then, I'll leave the Swallow here,' I said quietly and opened the door, making the little bells chime.

'Where are you going?' he called after me.

'Home,' I said without turning round. It was only when I was back in my flat that I realized I'd left the light blue paper umbrella lying on the counter.

The summer spread out over the city, the dry air turned dusty. The streets smelled of dogs and pre-cooked meals. I left the window open, even at night, the summer stole into the flat from outside and made it a part of the city. It was evening, already late, when the doorbell rang. Uli was standing in the dark hallway, casually leaning his shoulder against the wall. He grinned, and asked, 'Shall we have a drink?' I let him in, he rummaged in his shoulder bag and produced an old camera. 'What am I meant to do with that?' I asked him. He said, 'Cleaned up by Hoffmann, it's a good piece, keep it. I can't sell it anyway.' I took the camera and didn't know what to do with it. I put it in the kitchen. Uli followed me. He pulled two beer bottles from his bag.

We had been sitting quite a while at the table in the kitchen when suddenly a loud wail, like singing, came from the yard.

'Neukölln's a great place to live,' Uli said, and didn't laugh. I went into the bedroom, where you can look out over the whole yard. I saw a man lying on his back in front of the dustbins, surrounded by three women. Uli came over to me at the window. I stepped back a bit. 'Well,' he said, 'he's had it.' 'You're kidding,' I whispered. 'He's dead,' Uli said matter-of-factly.

I closed the window quietly and carefully. The yard was lit by two bare lightbulbs. In the pale light the women knelt down and stood up again, they sang, they beat their hands in front of their faces. I leant against the pane and noticed Uli coming up behind me. 'He's just fallen over there,' I said. 'Kid,' Uli shouted, 'he's stone dead.'

'How undignified,' I said quietly, 'you don't die in front of the rubbish bins in a filthy yard like this.' 'Dying is always undignified,' Uli said, 'and in any case, you never know where it'll get you.' The singing echoed between the walls, one woman kept smoothing the man's hair out of his eyes. She rocked her torso slowly back and forth.

After a while paramedics rushed into the yard, followed by a younger woman, they knelt down in front of the man. Their jackets glowed in the light from the lightbulbs. The women's singing died away. I moved back from the window, my back bumped against Uli's stomach. He put his hands on my hips. 'Maybe,' he said quietly, 'there's a small chance in this case.'

The paramedics put the man on a stretcher, covered him with a blanket up to his chin and carried him out. Uli was still standing behind me. Lights had now come on in some of the windows of the houses opposite. Shadow figures gathered in the crossbars of the windows. 'Maybe,' I said and pulled away from Uli's hands. We stood facing each other. He looked at me for a long time. I looked down.

'Should I stay,' he asked quietly, 'or should I go?'

'Don't mind,' I said. He hesitated, walked around the room, unsure, picked up his jacket, held it in his hands. 'Stay,' I said and left the room, I wanted to be as far away from the yard as possible.

He came after me, stood in the hall and said, 'Marie.' He said my name like it was a statement and at the same time a curse. He just stood there and said, 'Marie.' I went back into the room, lay down on my front on the sofa and breathed into the cushions. That's how I stayed lying and fell asleep at some point.

I woke up, not for long, and didn't know how long I'd been asleep. I noticed that Uli was sitting next to me on the sofa, his hand was resting on my neck, his fingers were touching my skin. I opened my eyes just a crack. It was dark in the room, I could smell the unwashed fuzz of his jumper.

I stayed where I was on the sofa. In the early morning I woke up with an aching back and went to lie down in bed. Uli was fully dressed and turned to face the wall when I got under the covers. We didn't touch. We got up around midday and I looked out the window onto the yard. It looked the same as always, dirty around the rubbish bins, straggly bushes behind them.

'Well?' asked Uli.

'I might have just been dreaming,' I answered.

He said as he went, 'Come by the shop, if you fancy. For the Swallow, too.'

I said I'd think about it. Maybe I'd go away. 'Where?' he asked, astonished.

'I don't know,' I said, 'just away.'

He looked back up the stairwell once, as if he wanted to capture an image of me. He raised his hand briefly. It was a strangely half-hearted, incomplete gesture.

It was only later, much later, that I recalled that my father had once said: don't ever wait for the swallows, they only come when you're no longer expecting them. It had been in the spring, on the dyke, I remember. Once, sometime in the winter, I had found a swallow's nest in the garden, it had fallen down, was just lying there among the thatch which dropped out of the roof. I had shown it to my mother and then put it in the shed. At the end of the winter I'd driven out to the dyke and had thrown it far out into the creek. I waited for a while, but it didn't resurface.

The Heart of the Republic

Fridolin Schley

> How glad I am to see the light
> I slept so peacefully last night
>
> (Child's prayer)

It was only on his way home, after Fabian had long since left the Palace behind, exiting on the Spree side, that he was struck by how exhausted he was and by the fact that he hadn't spoken to any of the other visitors.

Fabian had the feeling that it was only a caprice of his poor sense of direction that had led him there. On one of his evening strolls through the city centre, which, despite the spaciousness of the streets, seemed to close in on him threateningly, particularly as darkness fell, he had soon lost his way in the Scheunenviertel and, to stem his rising panic, had fixed his gaze on the flashing coloured lights of the TV tower on Alexanderplatz, hurrying towards them as if drawn by a spell, without paying any attention to the traffic or the lively bustle in the side streets. As a child he must once have known these streets inside out, something which seemed to him now like an opaque trick played by his memory.

The sight of the dark expanse of the Lustgarten and the baroque grandeur of the Berliner Dom finally calmed him so he was able to stand still for a second, look around and recognize that the Palace of the Republic on the other side of the street was not, as he assumed, lurking in the darkness like a long-abandoned factory building but rather that light was shining through some of the windows onto the former Schlossplatz and that in front of the entrance a large cluster of people had formed, which at that very moment started to move and surged into the building.

Of course the Palace had been Fabian's destination from the outset. In a childish way he felt quite daring, when he reached the end of the queue and joined in line without knowing what awaited him and he heightened this pleasant sense of risk even more by nodding in friendly fashion to the couple in front of him who were elegantly dressed and he wished them 'a pleasant evening'. The man returned the greeting and said, 'Wagner à la

GDR, that could be interesting,' and Fabian even acknow-
ledged the attendant checking the tickets on the door with
a knowing smile, and then walked without being detained
into the entrance hall. The public was already spreading
out; some people were milling around by a temporary
metal railing and were watching the musicians tuning up
their instruments on the other side, who had gathered at
the foot of a grand stone staircase, others like him made
their way further into the room and into a dimly lit
corridor, whose dimensions he couldn't make out.

Fabian remembered that this catacomb-like storey had
originally not been open to the visitors to the Palace, but
had instead been used as storage and cloakroom space with
its many small rooms. The ceiling above the main corridor
was suspended only just above head height, he felt his way
along the cold damp walls, with the old gas pipes which ran
on the left and right like veins, putting each foot down
cautiously and didn't let the man in front of him get more
than three metres ahead. Whatever you do, don't get left
behind down here, he thought, no-one said a word any
more, behind him only the scraping sound of footsteps, the
increasingly distant discord of the instruments and they, the
visitors, were like prisoners escaping together. They reached
the first floor via a staircase which opened up out of
nowhere on the right-hand side and, relieved, entered a
broad room which they could hardly take in at a glance,

which seemed to have corners on all sides that opened out into other rooms and the room's height stood in opposition to the constrictive narrowness of the entrance area. From here, Fabian reckoned he knew, stairs and lifts had once led to all floors and linked the Great Room with the People's Chamber. For some minutes he stood on the spot, simply turning his head to look all around. The walls had for the most part been torn down, the whole room was a fleshless skeleton, crossed by weight-bearing steel girders and metal poles; of the more than a thousand globe lights which had once lit up the room only rusting iron fittings remained, marked with yellow symbols and numbers at regular intervals. Fabian wasn't able to take in the whole room, in the distance the contours became too fluid. The pattern of collapsed brick walls, individual columns sticking up, the sills and panes of the high-set windows at the side, in addition to the faint, diffuse light in which silhouettes of visitors occasionally appeared briefly and disappeared again, created an impression of great indistinctness. In the distance even bigger rooms seemed to loom in a blur, there were rows of pillars and brickwork arches, which supported the upper level. In the warped floor he could make out patches of the black and white marble mosaic that at one time must have added to the effect of splendour—balls, conventions, and concerts had all taken place here—and all of a sudden, after Fabian had torn himself away and was wandering round aimlessly, it seemed incomprehensible to him that this building could have succumbed to the destruction so completely in such a short space of time, that it could stand here in the middle of a growing, constantly evolving city and at the same time continue to disintegrate from the inside out, and he thought about the many memories of this place, its stories, which, given it had no memory of its own, were being consumed together with its interior without ever having been heard or recorded.

The music must have started a while ago, for the visitors now came rushing out of the mist from all around the room towards the balustrade, from where they could see into the lobby. That was where the majority of the orchestra and the conductor had taken up their places. But after a few minutes Fabian could hear, between the strings and brass, growing clearer, a scratchy drone, which sounded like an old record player arm had come out of the groove, and the dull thud of electronic bass. He looked around and spotted more musicians on other floors; a DJ wearing headphones on a ledge on the third floor was actually using a record player. The music seemed to do what Fabian himself had failed to do shortly before, it seemed to be able to reach into the whole building, into every corner and moreover to fill the space.

Gradually some of the listeners broke away from the crowd by the balustrade and continued their tour. The movement of the visitors, their wandering, must have been an integral part of the concept for the evening, because Fabian couldn't see any seating anywhere, apparently people were meant to walk around freely on the different levels during the concert, as if they were acting out in slow motion the proceedings of a ball from bygone parties in the Palace.

Fabian too had moved on, but soon stopped with a few others in front of a blown-up photograph displayed on an easel, which he stared at for a long time before he recognized on it that very room, that is, the main foyer in which he was currently standing. The picture had been taken from an elevated position, probably from the second floor, and showed from above and at an angle the brightly lit dance hall, in which small groups of people wearing dark evening dress stood together in conversation, some were frozen in the middle of a dance step, others were sitting round the edges on the leather furniture, raising glasses of Sekt, or were leaning against the massive columns in the second floor gallery, looking down at the dancers with detachment. A warm orange light shone from the spherical lamps on the ceiling into the hall, which was adorned with a tall sculpture made of glass and steel in the centre of the room, and Fabian lifted his head time and again to try to orientate himself in the room using the photograph, wondered where the sculpture must have stood and which spot in the picture he was standing on now.

Fabian must have raised and lowered his head for a while, to compare the photo of the former splendour with the state of dilapidation, with the effect that afterwards he had no memory of the concert itself and he could only assume that there had been a constant stream of visitors who walked past him, stood next to him for a moment, glanced at the photograph and then went on their way, while he stood there almost motionless. The *Glass Flower,* his father had said, was nearly five metres tall and like so much had simply disappeared after the Palace was closed; works of art had also been stolen from the gallery, large oil-paintings by Willi Sitte and Arno Mohr, which had been put on display in the very first exhibition, the now famous, 'Are Communists allowed to dream?'

Fabian had gone on a bit further and ended up on the second floor via a staircase, from where you entered the former Great Hall, which surpassed even the lobby in height and length.

Eighteen metres high, 67 metres long, his father had explained over and over again, conventions and political gatherings had been the main events here, but thanks to the technical construction and fittings the hall had also been used for balls, banquets, and all sorts of orchestra concerts. The seating capacity which could be changed at the touch of a button, indeed, the completely flexible functionality and aesthetics of the space had been the only one of its kind in the world; at conventions 5,000 people could be seated at a writing desk, for dance competitions on the other hand they had raised the six swivel-mounted seating levels to sixty degrees and lowered by nearly six metres 24 ceiling plates which had built-in lighting bridges. The mechanism was still intact, so too the moving stages in the old theatre in the fourth floor, but to maintain technical functioning permanently these needed to be moved at least once a week, and the last official use had been some (and here Fabian's father looked shocked every time) twelve years ago.

Fabian returned to the first floor to hear the music better, but he kept stopping abruptly, to look in one direction or another and to recall his father's explanations.

His own memories of the Palace of the Republic were limited to a few short moments and impressions and even with these Fabian didn't know for certain whether he had really experienced them himself or if they were not rather a product of his imagination and his research, a montage of the many photos and reports he had looked at and read during recent months. His mother had told him that they had come here on a few Sundays before the fall of the Wall, his parents, his sister, and him. They simply walked past the queue and went in, were greeted politely at the entrance, and if there was one thing he could still picture quite clearly it was the moment when they entered and walked up the stairs inside the entrance—how with every step the immense scale of the room revealed itself, as if you were leaving the real world for a private place, a world created by his father.

For Fabian's father had designed the Palace and built it, not on his own of course, but he had been part of the collective of architects who had been commissioned after the ministerial decision in 1973 to build a house for the people, the topping out ceremony had taken place as early as the end of 1974 and the official opening of the Palace had been in April 1976—Fabian wouldn't be born until much later. His father had also been involved in other, less well-known (and therefore still standing, as before) official state buildings, the Stelzenhaus on Alexanderplatz or the GDR Embassy in Budapest. In the eighties he had been the chief architect for blocks of flats in Marzahn and Hellersdorf, but the Palace was undoubtedly his masterpiece, and these days Fabian was sometimes annoyed that he hadn't been able to experience and appreciate his father's work properly as a child back then. At school and elsewhere, the fact that his father had been the architect of the Palace of the Republic wasn't supposed to be more important than working in a factory and even his father, when he was at home and not in his study, the floor of which was always completely covered with unrolled paper plans and drawing material, had very rarely spoken about his job.

In fact it was only in the last months, Fabian thought, since the thing with his heart had become so serious, that his father had repeatedly started to do so, lying on his sick bed, had even asked him to go down to the garage and look out the old plans and bring them to his bedside. It hadn't been the right time before, after all his father had had plenty of work even in reunified Berlin, many others had had a much harder time. There hadn't been any unemployed architects round here for a long time.

But he had never quite recovered from the asbestos— in both senses. His father had had practically nothing to do with the scandal, the tests and the removal (others had been in charge of the façade's insulation, the question of responsibility had never come as far as him), but when the proposal to tear down the Palace had started doing the rounds and was being taken more and more seriously, that was the only time that Fabian heard his father shout and curse out loud. And the fact that shortly afterwards the pains in his chest had got worse and he himself had grown weaker and weaker and soon couldn't get out of bed, you couldn't seriously call that coincidence. Then, during the three months of care and convalescence, his father had mentioned the Palace increasingly frequently—the fact that at the time it was said to be the most modern edifice for culture in Europe (and that despite the fact that the GDR state was practically broke), at least as far as the interior design was concerned, the world had never seen such cleverly designed multifunctionality before. His father recalled the details of the development ever more precisely and, nearly every day, if he wasn't too weak to speak, he would explain to his family once again that they had taken their direction from Schinkel's idea of the house of the people, parliamentary debates and restaurants for the public under one roof, plus bowling alley, theatre, and art galleries. No-one had ever dared to do something like that before.

By this point in time the decision had long since been made to demolish the Palace in order to rebuild the Prussian Stadtschloss and the stripping of the interior in the course of the asbestos removal was nearly complete, and yet on good days they could not stop his father from looking for alternative solutions in textbooks and endless telephone conversations with old colleagues. Sometimes he got so worked up that they had to put him back in bed, which took all three of them and nearly required force, and take the books out of his hands, however much he struggled and berated his family, they had to understand, he said, there were totally new possibilities, the USA had tested the Thermo-Shield in outer space, did they not understand what that meant, sealing in rather than removing, locking in the poison rather than ripping it out, keeping the Palace rather than destroying it, and they pulled the covers up to his chin and tried to calm him, your heart, you need to sleep, father, think of your heart. Then he would sink, exhausted, into a half-sleep, sometimes for days, and the only sign that he was still alive was the regular rise and fall of the bedcovers on his chest. You don't kill a sick man, you treat him, he murmured, when he next was able to speak.

Fabian didn't actually believe you could say there was a direct link between the demise of the Palace and his father's heart problems, because the first symptoms had appeared much earlier, but the chronological coincidence was strikingly clear. Years before, while routine tests were being carried out in the course of the asbestos scandal, his father had been diagnosed with signs of silicosis, but the external symptoms like dry-coughing, bloody expectorate and shortness of breath had faded over time and had only reappeared after years of living symptom-free (and professional success), together with coronary heart disease. They had moved to Bavaria years ago, for the curative air.

According to the doctors in Starnberg, chronically inflamed lungs had gradually affected his heart over the years and weakened it, further risk factors such as raised cholesterol, the stress of work, and the fact his father was overweight had all led to a dramatic narrowing of the coronary blood vessels, insufficient infusion of blood and finally to asymptomatic myocardial ischaemia, the family must reckon with further heart attacks. The doctors advised against an operation, in the particular circumstances the outcome would almost certainly not be successful, now it was the family's turn to ask, and after Fabian's father himself had repeatedly pressed him on it, the smug chief physician had said reflectively, with his head to one side, perhaps three months left, but with the best will in the world they couldn't know precisely. That was on 16 June.

Fabian had stopped again in front of an almost completely darkened room, he couldn't have said how long he had been wandering around, the memories had so engulfed him that he had nearly forgotten the place which only moments before had so overwhelmed him and interested him in every detail. With his hands behind his back he had walked blindly from room to room and he even seemed to be further away than ever from the music. Now he was standing in the Linden restaurant, he knew because his father had told him that the coloured tapestries on the walls had been one of the main artistic attractions in the Palace, here people could sit plate by plate next to party comrades, directly below the conference rooms in the People's Chamber suite.

So it had been 16 June. He knew so precisely because the date of the diagnosis, together with the doctor's roughly estimated timescale which put a limit on the time remaining, was of decisive significance, overshadowing everything in the following weeks. His mother had been the first to come out of the shocked trance (and once, in the kitchen, had said, with a pathos which was completely unlike her, 'Now we'll strike back') and had taken leave of all her other everyday duties for three months. The days were structured in accordance with the strict exigencies of the illness, from now on the whole family took their meals, based on a low-fat diet, around the sick bed and his mother, his sister, and he himself had taken turns to wash, feed, and talk to his father, who got weaker and paler by the day. Some weeks, as a rule directly after hearing reports about developments concerning the future of the Palace on the radio (for which reason they soon removed the radio from his room), his father fell into a sleep-like state and was only fully conscious for short periods of time at most.

The emaciation of his body proceeded at such a pace that the sick room had to be fitted out with all sorts of technical equipment which enabled the patient to be treated with nitro solutions and artificial nutrition. Soon his father lay among a jungle of cables, wires, and tubes, and from time to time Fabian was amazed that, despite being barely responsive for days and weeks at a time and lying in a room completely cut off from the outside world, his father was able to keep the whole family running round the clock. They worked shifts, relieving each other day and night; the data for the heart rhythm and pump volume had to be noted and conveyed to the doctor, beta-blockers and aggregation inhibitors needed to be administered almost hourly (to counter the patient's low resistance), the room temperature was checked regularly and the sweat-drenched sheets changed.

They had felt like performers in a succession of scenes, when one after the other they performed the movements which had soon become routine on the stage of the sick room, but what Fabian liked most of all the tasks was reading to his drowsing father from the paper in the morning (he and his sister had been excused from school and community service[1] for three months). Even the two or three games of chess which lasted for weeks had had an extraordinarily calming effect, a feeling of being deeply connected with the sick man. Fabian knew how crass it sounded, but in retrospect he had the impression that ultimately it was the prophesied and therefore manageable time period of three months, as well as the date of death calculated thereby (16 September), which had made it

---

[1] Civilian national service, an alternative to the compulsory stint in the armed forces.

possible for him to get through this exceptional situation with unfailing strength.

But then something unforeseen had happened: after about six weeks his father's condition began to improve significantly. One morning they found him wide awake and sitting upright in bed, he asked for fried eggs and coffee for breakfast and a week later his waking phases won out for the first time since his collapse, something which the doctors said was unusual and remarkable.

The family now had to adapt to his father's constant progress. As he recovered he wanted to be kept occupied all day, board games, skat, and soon they had to carry the television upstairs, even though his mother would not relinquish control over the viewing, no thrillers and no tearjerkers, she said, and under no circumstances political shows or news. And it was his mother who also insisted on sticking to the original timetable for treatment, too much of a good thing would be better than reproaching themselves at a later date, she argued, and his father had to subject himself even more frequently than before to stress radiography and X-ray examinations of the coronary blood vessels in the clinic, although he cried with pain when they injected the contrast agent via a catheter into his groin.

But overall he recovered a bit more every day, the first steps out to the garage and back turned into increasingly long walks during which he made plans for the future and began lectures about the history of architecture. However after a few sentences he always returned to the subject of the Palace of the Republic, he recalled the design phase, from decades ago, in the tiniest detail, names of long-forgotten work colleagues came to him and he dismissed with irritation Fabian's mother's attempts to calm him ('Please think of your heart for once, and of us!') and carried on with his explanations of the layout and functioning of the Palace. But after he had worked on them over and over for a few weeks, his words became less angry each time, until once, after he had given a long lecture with the expertise of a professor about the construction of the Great Hall, he said in an entirely unusual conciliatory tone, ach, what the hell, everything has its day after all, and no-one knew what to say to that.

After that Fabian's father never spoke again about the Palace of the Republic. Instead he started to take interest in his illness. He ordered piles of books on the internet about asbestos and other poisonous building materials, which his family lugged into his sick room and which he read until late in the night. Fabian's mother however still refused to take down the drip and testing equipment and even when his father had started rehabilitative physiotherapy, press-ups, and gentle weight-training she had such a fit of crying and ranting that eventually he agreed to an elaborate interval therapy in which the blood vessels were expanded using lasers and wire mesh.

His father made drawings of the tiniest silicon particles and copied them in felt-tip onto large posters which were hung above his bed. Over breakfast he held forth, explaining that the mineral asbestos took its name from a small Russian mountain village and even in ancient times it had been used in the manufacture of candle wicks and cloth, and he spent a whole weekend tapping for traces of asbestos in places in the flat that seemed suspicious—ventilation ducts, floor covering as well as the casing on the ceiling and the heating.

In the end Fabian's father had made an almost complete recovery from his illness, he conducted long telephone conversations with his office and was involved in work decisions; the doctors were therefore all the more surprised when they heard from his mother at the beginning of September that her husband had agreed to the family's request that he undergo open heart surgery for a bypass. Were they aware that normally this was a last resort ... would a preliminary ion beam treatment perhaps not be preferable ... they must warn them that the mortality rate still stood at 20 per cent ...

But the operation passed without complications and was pretty much a textbook example, the senior physician announced; the test results were startling, he said, they had not only been able to stabilize the patient's heart function but for reasons still unexplained had even been able to improve it.

Fabian's father was discharged from hospital as early as 10 September, not long afterwards he was able to embark on easy cross-country runs without becoming short of breath and even the day before his death, which came as a complete shock, he had told the family of his intention to step down from his managerial role at work in order not to jeopardize unnecessarily his health and the new sense of togetherness which the family had discovered over the past three months. His heart had given him a real shot across the bows and signalled that the time had come.

When he really thought about it, Fabian mused, his father, who was found by his mother a few hours later, on the morning of 16 September, had died on the very day he was completely better. The circumstances remained unexplained, the inquest was still ongoing, and their grief was now also so crippling (particularly for his mother), that the surprising result of the first autopsy had not been able to elicit a single word of reaction from them. The doctors' opinion was that the original diagnosis had been inaccurate, if not incorrect, his father had not had a heart condition at all, which accounted for the otherwise inexplicable speed of his recovery, if not for the primary illness. In fact to date they had been unable to identify even the faintest sign of disease (aside from chronically inflamed vocal chords which were the result of childhood diphtheria which had only partially healed). But in the end the further findings relating to the cause of his father's death were immaterial for Fabian and indeed were almost inconvenient, for it was grotesque whichever way he looked at it.

factions

Kathrin Röggla

—there's no such thing as hard house, he says categorically, and carries on rolling his cigarette. hardly a flying start to the conversation. there's no such thing as hard house, he says, there's just hard trance, hard house doesn't exist, he should know, not as music anyway, there's the label, yes—

so he's woken up again, sven has surfaced from his melancholy again, and the object-beckoning starts up again immediately: no, i don't measure up to my t-shirt, it washes me out, clothes certainly give you plenty to think about, oh yes.

in the 90s it was the 70s again for two years, but that wasn't long enough to bring back the 90s, after that things went backwards again, towards the 50s if not further, where the guys and dolls blossomed separately, scuppered each other: battleships! and soon the 20s will be taking hold in berlin again, that's what's chic now. if things start to shrink and shrink until one day they're gone completely, then that will definitely have been the 20s. advance ticket sales for that have been going well already.

but we're stuck on: there's no such thing as hard house.
—what?
—i mean, as music. hard trance, sure, but not hard house, he goes back to his cigarette, you must mean the label, harthouse
—no, i mean hard house the music.

just because he doesn't like hardcore music, it doesn't exist. just because he apparently once worked in a record shop, he always has to know better, he must have been given an extra canal in his ear, he hears things differently to us, you see: he hears twice as much and twice as fast and always knows what it is: his ear is linked directly to his brain, not like it is for us, for us sounds just come and then just go again.
—what are you like, okay, then there is such a thing as hard house.

two drive past in a car. two always drive past in a car at such moments and always have something important to discuss, so we go with them. happens increasingly frequently, meeting two people in a car, it's rapidly on the increase in this city. but a car isn't really a suitable sociable place, particularly not for a juicy argument. whatever: on the back seat you can rewind a bit, with strategic comrades and alliances: well personally i'd go via the oberbaumbrücke.

—and why not straight to jannowitzbrücke, or do you want to go to friedrichshain?

—god no!

driving through the city: do we to go to mitte now, or not? nah, the hauptbahnhof: there's meant to be some venue there, between the building site and the post office

—never heard of it.

—yeah well you read the wrong newspaper.

bloke sitting next to you, see how he laughs: always laughs at his own jokes without telling them first, and the one in the front, see how he's driving: is tripping or not, the passerby hurrying by won't wonder for long, because he doesn't really exist either. for crying out loud, what's going on out there? frenetic silence, everything's empty.

'oi, drive carefully like.' but everyone knows shouting from the back never helps. outside it's still köpenicker straße, jeez it's long today. and then *heinrich heine*, the fischerinsel, *leipziger*: haven't we seen that before some-where? 'hey, where exactly are you heading?'

sven, sven, how will things end with us, where are things going tonight? that's easy: past the empty areas around friedrichstraße, across the whole wasteland of investment opportunities—'and are they still tapping phones here?' comes from the front: martin, also present, laughs: 'would love to know what you can hear there.' brand spanking new silence, i presume, you don't step onto this planet out of choice. today you've gotta be happy if the architects take account of the 'needs of the area'— but who wants to think about residential quarters these days, we don't anyway, we're off in the car aren't we, and chris still hasn't calmed down, we can't get him to slow down. so let's move the architecture debate onto other things: 'turn the music down! we can't hear ourselves speak.'

outside is berlin mitte from the road: motorway halves rather than halves of houses, and halves of houses rather than faces on a saturday afternoon-to-be on the spree . . . though there's nothing more to see, everything's gone, disappeared in the direction of the capital, squares swept bare . . . what can you do there? on the other hand martin now stages some pop-theory-mix, yeah in a kind of voodoo style he discusses the situation, afterwards you don't know what's what, where's the seriousness, where's the fun, where's beginning, where's end: 'hey, what are you on about again?'—but apparently for me asking cool questions with cool timing isn't possible, that's how he's looking at me: 'was only joking.'

okay then: martin, barely thawed out, puts together some other pop-theory-mix in the front, that's what it's like in berlin, if you're not in cologne, if you're not in munich, then you're sitting in a car in berlin—no, people don't sit in cars in berlin.—alright, you're sitting some-where else, like in *discount,* that shifts too, you can kick off there too, for fun, as you like: who's coming with, then?

—no-one!

—okay, fine, stick little stars on your forehead (the eighties are coming back!) and while you're at it draw up strategies for the new millennium, not in some dark and dingy dive, no, it needs to be in some club for the shock-wave existence, one which semi fits the early eighties design. but here we've got something more undefinable with diametrically opposed light shows—somewhere in the depths of a room there's always a dj these days, so there must be one here somewhere, but we don't find it, and that tips us over the edge: the music is playing itself and it's so loud ...

and yet dj is the number one call, number one calling, there's pretty much nothing else—rubbish!—jeez, was just meant 'as a metaphor', just an image—but almost everything these days is meant just as an image, 'of course the world consists of images', that's martin, 'i mean, let's not kid ourselves', he starts again, 'we're setting up clichés that we move around, rhythmic, pictorial, formal clichés'.

at the same time we're still sitting at the same place, the houses aren't collapsing, the good walls are still standing. nothing much going on, basically the joint is empty. 'it is wednesday evening', starts up again. but wherever you go it's always a total sideshow for some main event which is going off somewhere else, no-one lets on where, you always only find out afterwards...

jeez, the pop faction always turn up everywhere all the time, but what's pop at a distance elsewhere is pap at a distance here, you hold it in front of your face so as to create some difference, you can hire it here (for DM3.50!—that's mad!), so you can be somewhere else when you look. the pill faction's coming up more now though, they're roaming around, half-naked, it's just their faces that appear in front of us. grin at us. and off they go through mitte, grinning at people, and they've already gone right through you.

personally i've never liked taking drugs, me personally, kerstin says now, sips her wine—who's kerstin? you might well ask—correct! well spotted! kerstin doesn't belong here either, she's sitting in one of the many restaurants near here and wants to have her say, wants to be there, part of the party in the hackesche höfe, as people call all these places here, ha-kke-sche-hööööfe! where all they do is sit and make sure they've got the right thing. yup, globalization winners, you wouldn't have thought it but they exist, here among us. you can touch them, you can speak to them, sometimes they even answer, these ones don't though, cos we're gone again—off to the next stop. the bitching faction (martin must have stayed here), they just bitch around, bitch and don't get anything, they always know everything better in advance, but every now and then they run out of themes: let's get out of here, they say then... then a little bit further on there's the survival faction (chris is in here, we assume), they don't take any notice of what's around them, they're just trying to get a handle on their own situation—

—stop!

—what?

—they're just laying people off here. let's get out of here!

he's right, he's right, but there's no way out of the 1990s, unless you go via yorckstraße, hasenheide, karl-marx-straße, buckower damm, you're well out of it then, between the onion gardens and the allotment plots—yes, a new reckoning of time begins between the summerhouses and the canals—but we don't even have a car, we've lost the others, and we're probably looking in the wrong place, more like standing around outside the apartment blocks on alex. and no-one comes out and wants to talk, they all stay sitting upstairs. yup, on the sixth floor there really is a tv window, they're all holed up, watching target telly! lifelong learning! or 'let's visit andy and grit'. but even they don't open the door to us, just carry on their mara-thon-couple-living, you can't open the door there any more, everyone knows—instead they are carrying their own 1990s, schlepping their private 1990s straight through the living room, that takes a lot of strength, but: what is at stake! because sometimes the little 1990s turn into the big 1990s, take over the space, stand there in the middle of the room, till they burst, scatter over everyone standing around—

—yes, you suddenly age a few years here.

—and in the end it's you hanging around in there.

—we've been watching the process for ages.

—what now?

in a situation like that you can never think of anything, to begin with you're just standing next to other people who seem to be waiting for the night bus, which definitely ought to come any second now. standing there with these figures: drunks, punks, students, tramps or other people and staring at some building opposite, a building site probably with a large billboard on the fence with the new office and residential block on it. to begin with you have conversations like, not to worry, there'll be something temporary along again. something temporary, and suddenly everyone has heard about it. temporary, ephemeral, passing—it's a process! kingly words for the outgoing 1990s!—not true!—what?—well, soon the city will be finished and nothing will change any more—something like that. but there are always spontaneous reactions, they have always turned up again: even in these latitudes, in this climate, even in a situation like this.

and then he started this subversion terror again. was only to be expected that he would get caught up again in his subversion terror: secret language on! after today no-one will understand me any more!—and that's probably what happened, and he'll have ended up in some kind of hippy faction: queer fish, fishing in troubled waters, I always say. think they can outwit the system with their secret languages, secret books, secret codes...

no, I say: and then he turned his subversion terror on: best to play it safe—'nothing to do with you!' there's no way out of the 1990s, you'll have to get past me first, that's what he looked like suddenly... and I just laughed at him...

and then he said something like: setting boundaries, being the boundary. i didn't really understand anyway... suddenly he didn't want to be alone any more... alone? i asked him that too, you see, even then i didn't understand what he was on about.

ach yes: you just can't call a spade a spade, he said to me then and went.

i didn't believe a word he said.

no, i've no idea where he is now. no, you probably know that better than i do too.

on the way home there's the lime blossom again, leaving a film on the street, on the car roofs, windscreens, covering the city with their pattern, a script that's hard to decipher, secret language! it whispers something to us. 'the surface of the earth is romantic,' schlegel said, we just have to decipher it, but i can't do it very well on my own.

Berlin City Guide

Wladimir Kaminer

For some time now Russian travel agencies have sold Berlin as a kind of insider's tip for the rich. They say, you can have fun to die for there. In one Russian city guide for Berlin tour operators advertise with the slogan 'Hoist your own personal flag on top of the new German Reichstag—come and conquer Berlin!'

My old friend Sacha who is studying German at the Humboldt University was recently commissioned to update one of these Russian Berlin guidebooks. Nothing dramatic, just a few new insider tips like Potsdamer Platz and suchlike. He came to me in despair. Rich Russians don't have much time, which is why the old guidebooks mostly only schedule one- or at most three-day trips. Everything has to move quickly. On a five-day trip for particularly pedantic tourists, the traveller even has to go to hell, or rather Potsdam—outside Berlin. 'A fabulous landscape with many sculptures, takeaways and waterfalls' is how the Russian version reads on Potsdam. 'Particularly recommended is the *Schloss Sanssouci*, built in 1744 by King Frederick I. The canteen there is also worth a visit, for grilled pork with bacon dumplings and red cabbage with apple. The picture gallery in the castle is similarly worth seeing, some real Caravaggios and Raphaels are hung there, however they are not for sale. Please note: even in extreme thirst, do not drink from the waterfall, it may cause illness.'

The entries for the shorter trips are composed in the same tone, a mixture of pathetic art book and carefully put-together menu. For the one-day trip the speed increases enormously. The Russian runs from the Europa-Center to the KaDeWe,[1] to try the lobster there. The KaDeWe is rated 'superb' and 'particularly good value'. After that he goes to the Brandenburg Gate, which is described as a 'superb remnant of the Berlin Wall'. You should also have a bite to eat in the eastern half of the city. Because the 'German steaks', as the Russians call Bockwurst sausage, are 'superb' in the East too, and taste 'fantastic'. Although the wine is no longer 'as sweet as it

[1] Kaufhaus des Westens, the large (and expensive) department store near Zoo Station.

was before the Wall came down, which was really quite a long time ago now'. Next it's off to the Reichstag, where the Russian can hoist his own personal flag—whatever the writer meant by that.

So now Sacha had to think up something about Potsdamer Platz. The two of us sat in the kitchen all evening. Odd. We couldn't think of anything for Potsdamer Platz. 'A superb piece of the future in the heart of the old city?' I suggested in despair. The last time I was there I was approached by security guards three times in the space of half an hour. The first time my shoelace was undone and I had knelt down to tie it. The next moment an official was standing over me: 'What's going on?' 'Thanks, everything is fine,' I replied and walked off. Looking for the toilets I walked into one of those lovely apartment and leisure blocks which are everywhere around there. Another official appeared immediately: 'What's up?' 'Everything's cushty,' I said and left. 'Visit Potsdamer Platz, the Reich of the rich. In the bars and casinos here you can get rid of all your hard-earned cash quickly and with ease.' We left it at that. It had got late. We went out and dived into the depths of Prenzlauer Berg to get a drink.

Gina Regina

Ulrike Draesner

Saturday afternoon and for once it wasn't raining. When it rained, birch pollen tea flowed along the gutters, even in the city. Gina's brain hung down through her sinuses and nostrils, despite the break in the rain it tasted like a brew of birch pollen and itched hellishly. Spring had sprung, brandishing streamers of allergies. A cocktail on the skin, an extra little shot from Mother-Drug-Nature. Gina chose Volcano Red from the colour chart and sat down in the waiting room.

Neon green cranes swayed outside the window, frozen in crooked poses against which the afternoon red, a half-hearted attempt at an orgiastic glow, struggled painfully. Lacquered nipples were the latest trend, recently imported from Japan.

You didn't lacquer yourself, you went to get yourself lacquered, Volcano Red, for example. Gina's neighbour on the waiting bench was wearing bright yellow linen shoes. Gina was relieved, a woman like that wouldn't uncouple her from her little horse, her little heart, this Gordian, whose ears had a hole in the tip—a piece was missing, as if it had been gnawed off in the womb. Maybe that's why he was so cute: as compensation. He preferred white shirts over the Gordian breast, which was completely smooth and hairless and its sole purpose was to tie knots in the hearts of people like Gina by eagerly pressing sternum bones against each other. For weeks Gina had been standing before it, puzzled: what had happened? The sweet pea-blue eyes of this Him exuded, so you'd want nothing more than to suck at them, but before Gina could sink any further into her deliberations her name was called. A minute later she obediently plumped down into the lap of a curly black-haired titaness, who was already tenderly turning the spray-gun in her hand.

Gina was biting into the sugar bun she had just bought when one of the city's *Weltuntergang*-phrases was hurled at her: spare a euro?! She walked on, gestured back with her bun. The lacquer was tightening somewhat. The banks had been advertising top rates for weeks. Apparently the Germans had savings by the sockful at home, which now needed to go to the bank. Only yesterday Gina-la-Minna had waited for nearly an hour in the savings bank, but no-one had tried to deposit a savings sock, which she would have loved to see just the once. She sighed and took another bite of sugar bun. The rapprochement with the always Gordian-minded Gordy was also something that had to be enjoyed. Gina was studying Romance Studies with International Relations as a minor, and that was something that had to be financed. The nipple lacquer doubtless contributed towards international relations; so to an even greater extent did Gina's job of course.

Dot.com. Gina had found her employer, who was based in California, on the net. She knew any number of men with commitment phobia, they gave off clouds of untouch-ability and every three weeks they had an attack of good old Freudian panic. Which really ought to have passed by now, but hibernated in these men like a swarm of bees in a hollow tree trunk, specializing in all things nectaral: suck it up, then buzz off. Mother-Drug-Nature showed how.

And that was Gina's big break.

She turned the tables. A simple business process, which moreover was enjoyable. Turn your talent into a job, advised the employer in his welcome email. That was indeed the whole concept. And he gave her an address where she was to hand in what came in to her. The moon was hanging in the afternoon sky, prion yellow, by the time Gina finally rang Gordian's bell, by the time the lacquer was finally hard to the touch.

Oh what foolishness! exclaimed Gordian, seeing Gina without t-shirt. By which he wasn't referring to her, but to himself, as normally he protected himself out of panic (Gina out of routine). What foolishness! he exclaimed and took the condom out of the packet, but didn't roll it on. Gina dug her claws into his neck and didn't let go. It was, as almost always, over too quickly. Yet even while Gordian was still inhaling his usual half-time cigarette with his cola the trembling came back. Gina tasted the smoke in Gordian's mouth, felt the smooth skin on his chest. His ribs stretched way down, she gripped his belly right underneath them as he came.

He slept. Reginal, Gina shimmied into her jeans, *queen of matter*. She liked the bum-in-two-halves feeling in them, but stopped when the trousers touched her upper thigh. Ferdi, who would only answer to Gordian in the life he knew as his own, his sperm ran down her left thigh. He gave good spurt, Gordy in his section of cabbage green *Plattenbau*.[1] He was otherwise healthy too, she had made enquiries, that was part of her job and she took pride in doing it well. The fact that her heart was beating so hard wasn't part of the picture admittedly. Gina's favourite saying was: My men

---

[1] Prefabricated apartment blocks, usually in East Berlin.

wear either aftershave or me. But she didn't want to do it again, to let something of Gordian's go, though—it wasn't theft, strictly speaking. Admittedly she wouldn't ever give it back to him, but he would never miss it. And hadn't he given it to her, so to speak, for free? Gina thought it was perfectly cunning, the way the cranes around here rocked happily even on top of rubbish; unlike on Potsdamer Platz, they were camouflaged in colours of leaf rust. Yes, camouflage everywhere, even sperm wears a cap thought Gina, and took her jeans off again. Then she looked for her handbag.

Stasi scent samples supposedly still stood in old cellars, waiting for their techno discovery, and would carry on waiting because the spirit had been let out. They could be opened in a vacuum, 20-year-old nostal-GDR air would come pouring out into the city. Gina swore softly, because she couldn't find her good Gucci PVC piece, and at this juncture it would have been the end of the story, a typical afternoon stand, an intermezzo of sugar bun and sex, if it hadn't been for Gina's employer, if Gina hadn't glanced over again at the sleeping Gordian and if her eyes hadn't fallen on the orange handle of her handbag, poking out from under the bed.

Collect the sperm, Gina-Regina thought, still in out-look express, always on the lookout for a fast buck, and rummaged in her bag for the test tube. She hadn't wanted to do it, at least not with her heartbeat Gordian, but she did it! The exaggeratedly protein-rich fluid meant something to her; it came just at the right moment. Now the accomplished hand movements: booty in the bag, sperm in the crop.

Her heart was beating like mad. Carefully, and quite exhausted, Gina sat down on the edge of the bed by Gordian. Was this the content and the form was slopping around in the tube? There the genotype, here the phenotype and, somewhere in between, the clever reproductive rules for copying? Like in the *Tractatus*, where Lucky Ludwig saw the particles of language and reality becoming tiny, atomic, subatomic, cosmic! Today particles of genes and humans. The only thing that wasn't clear was who decides how they belong together. To explain the first thing about 'world togetherness', Gina giggled to herself, you need to factor in a lacquered nipple, which always gets forgotten. Gina was a special rank of head hunter, a sperm trapper in plain English. Wasn't prostitution. For one thing, she earned more: an order with her employer cost between 500 and 2000 dollars. She took 60 per cent, after all she could offer exceptional male specimens. As a rule they could precipitate several solutions from one of the contributions she extracted from a condom. For artificial insemination, which was the case here, you actually need much less sperm than with megalomaniac Mother Nature. Secondly, she sought out her men herself, only the best among her peers. For a fuck she could have almost anyone and word went round that she was a good one night stand, no drama afterwards, carries on saying hello on campus without any awkwardness, Gina, Regina of donations. Thirdly: there was no-one watching over her. When she got something she took it to the laboratory. Fourthly: it was illegal. An extra kick. The danger of any of the men she milked ever finding out was limited however, because of course she used made-up names. Gordian was called Ferdy Duke on the website (German with an American grandfather, a GI from the time of World War Two heroes, his mother conceived in '49, him in '78, young sperm all round). If any of them were still to find out and object, she would give him an ironic hard time, then dollarollover. But she'd got stuck on Gordian, because of the heart beating business. Gina groaned inwardly at herself, saw in her mind a beating little red heart, shaped like a piedmont cherry, dipped in chocolate, Mon Chéri.

Of course like everyone else she rejected retro values absolutely. And now this. Amour fou? Gina smoothed a blond hair from her decidedly high forehead, covered by an old-fashioned, therefore now cool again, fringe, and was glad that she had tested out all her sky-will-fall-on-my-head fears thoroughly in her comic years. What seemed like a waste of time then had in fact been preparation for life (children's famous instinct, as certain to hit the mark as pink marshmallows thrown into the mouth).

High time to head off, fluted-flirted Reginaldine to her Ferdy Duke, her Eldorado, in his ear, shaking his shoulder:

—I'm thirsty!

—really?

—!

—I'm coming,

he scrambled out of bed, his face lifted up, closer to Regina, no: just his mouth, his whole face was mouth, just lips, so red, how did he do that, two large balconies, like in a film, zoom, towards Regina, or did she bend over, whatever, they met, fitted, lips away, it tasted of Gordian-sleep-sex, of peace, childlikeness, it tasted, Ginaregina! like milk, for seconds, that couldn't be, yes, tasted, slurped, licked, really, yes, indeed, a kiss on his lovely lips, on his ... yet normally she never kissed.

The basket chairs creaked gently in Dante under the S-Bahn arches, which groaned and echoed like the inside of a hollowed-out breast. Gina was shocked, just for a second. They were visiting Hackescher Markt, the city's valley of roses,[2] once a deserted wasteland, now perfectly

---

[2] Rosenthal, valley of roses; Rosenthalstraße is a street in the Hackescher Markt area.

redeveloped, stooled and cooled, cherry trees in front of renovated walls. Spring air by the gallon. Regina was thinking about nights she had frozen here, bars appearing, bars disappearing, the appearance of the toytown house fronts, always the same man selling lilac in May in the exit from the S-Bahn, the one tree left standing, the underground cables, the latest trends in the shop on the round corner, the tubes of lycra clothing her body. Gordian was thinking about what it means to reproduce a human being in engineering terms, a second-degree act of genius therefore. For the brain alone you need, with the latest minichips, an area only the size of Greater London, said Gordian, who was studying mechanics, but because a brain only functions in relation to others, they would need to be built too, so the whole planet would be completely covered with engineering just to make *one* person function. Now those were truly Alexandrian plans! The sword which would sever a knot as small but as well guarded as Gordian's heart, however, was still to be found. Ginna-la-Minna felt her breath, she would rather have been sucking in Gordian air. The plastic tube with the drops of sperm she had collected clunked against her mobile and the morning air stored in her handbag. She had made enquiries with California. The impurities the sperm picked up dripping down her skin could be filtered out with no difficulty. Gina sneezed; the pollen tickled.

Berlin in the Spring. Pink messengers shot by, mail amazons on mortal trips to the sound of the soft clicking of
their fully digitalized 27-Shimano gearshifts. Vanilla-
scented white-varnished nails grasped the rubber bands
on the handlebars. Sometimes the amazons folded their
arms in an X over the handlebars or tucked their thumbs
under their forefingers, just as the Sphinx in Giza had
rested her claws on top of each other. Gordian sucked
contentedly at his Bloody Cola Mary. Gin was not necessarily the thing. A few neon blue tubes imitated the flight
of swallows and decorated window displays with patterns
of midges. Spring, spring, swing your band of Visa-gold.[3]

Gina-Benigna slurped at her rum and coke, amused.
Didn't her work bring together national and international,
typical-German and individualistic, in the most beautiful
way? On www.rose-angels.com you could view what she
donated; there you could apply for sperm samples, clients
worldwide, for whatever conception you liked.

To Einstein, Gina cheerfully raised her glass to her un-
knotted, unsuspecting Gordian: Einstein said you must
make things as easy as possible, but no easier! At that she
showed Gordian her tongue and let him check for dimples
at its edges. It was one of the most intimate acts possible, she
saw up his nostrils as he was doing it. Everything about this

---

[3] A play on Mörike, 'Frühling lässt sein blaues Band' (Spring swings its blue
band).

man seemed to be one whole, a connectedness. So he really was human after all, however often he claimed not to know the room in which his Gordian heart lay in a glass cabinet. But Giny-Riny insisted, blushing slightly, in tender moments, that she tarried there, and had been there with him time and again, amour, fou, folle, she thought. The room was real, as real as the inside of her handbag, lined with fox-fur or even lynx.

Ginnina would have sighed, had that not been so uncool.

—Can I take a photo of you?

She saw him on the screen of her hand-size digi-cam, on which reality appeared once more and even more real, at a safe distance, she saw him smiling there.

—Well stand up then!

The green of the trees in the background suited him. Full body shot. It didn't have to be naked photos, quite the opposite, www.rose-angels.com wasn't about sex, it was about reproduction. *Attractive male German, white, 25 y.o., Mathematical Engineer, IQ between 120–140* (there was a box to tick for that), *height: 185 cm, weight: 73 kg.*

In the meantime Gina had ordered a Screwdriver, one of her attempts at self-irony, the drink was known as vodka and orange. In her handbag the tenth Ferdy-tube sloshed around, all the little microscopic fishies in it. Although she had wanted to stop doing it, really stop, with him at least. The other times she had emptied the condom in Gordian's bathroom already, sometimes she had wrapped it up and 'disposed' of it at home, meaning to put it in the fridge or taken it to the laboratory straight away, from where the little tubes were flown to the US, deep-frozen, normally the same day. And today—again. She had to do it. If you can't eat it, smoke it or stroke it, was written large above Gina's bed. It's probably there. It was always there.

Gordian was smoking, Reginni had peeled him a rizla for a joint. He was still thinking about Einstein; even the fact that he tried to study some philosophy was on the rosy angel site, which he knew nothing about. Gina's central surrogate brain was starting to throw up odd images on her video system. Should she tell him? Reveal who she was—no, not that; but maybe what she did? In a sudden rush Gina squeezed Gordian's hand more firmly than she meant to. He took it as a sign that they should set off. Essay due on Monday, Gina had told him some hours earlier; in fact she had another appointment at 8 p.m.

Berlin in the Spring. A belching St Bernard with a little bottle of rum round its neck ran through a glacier in Karwendel, searching for a man with overblown Otzi ambitions, while on the Finnish–Russian border a few spruce trees were bathing their last needles in the unsetting sun. In Osterwalde a biologist shook millimetre-long bugs into a water glass, put them under a microscope and was meticulously sketching the mutations she found. A rootling ray in the Sargasso sea was sniffing at a post-Soviet U-boat where they were playing chess with figures cast in shiny pewter, when there were several flashes from the shop that G&G were strolling past, because a six-year-old thief wearing a black leather jacket broke through the barrier. Later all they will see on the picture is his mop of hair.

—Funny, Gina said to Gordian, whose trousers were already starting to bulge slightly again, that another person has a different heart to you. It's the first thing you see on the ultrasound of a foetus. It beats unbelievably fast: *punctum saliens*, Aristotle said, he studied it in hens' eggs!

But feelings don't have their seat in the heart, biologists had known that for a long time, only language hadn't kept pace with the times. Gina glanced across at Gordian quickly, he smiled, he had just opened his mouth to answer, when she pushed him away:

—You only fancy me for my lacquered nipples! I don't want to see you any more.

Whatever: she really meant it. It would have been better for him, and possibly for her too, if they split up here. Gordian replied simply:

—oh come on!

Gordian didn't fall for the authenticity trip (feelings, not sex) for a second and put his arm round Gina's shoulders. She dropped the attempt at something beyond rose-selling dot.com, relieved. Why bother with internal conflict? They were open, they were in a hurry, they regularly shaved their private parts, sported lizard tattoos with red eyes. They stood by the Treptowers, some youngsters toasted marshmallows there every afternoon, two giant aluminium men full of holes hobbled in the middle of the river, made from GDR money, two who always got wet feet.

Berlin in the Spring. If it all worked out she would have made a pretty penny this weekend, it would have been worth investing in the lacquer. Ginnina lay on the sofa in her flat and entwined her arms in the X-shape that she so admired on the bike messengers. It was reminiscent of the double helix. Gordian's tube was carefully stored in its special freezer, which froze at 90 below. When she had got home she had kissed the tube and decided to keep it. Her very special gift to Gordian. Exhausted by this decision, Gina was now lying on her sofa, before she had to head out just before eight to her rendezvous with Mike. A seagull carved the corners of a triangle in the sky, a dirty cloud scudded hurriedly after. Getting the munchies, the presenter on NTV said. Is the aroma typical of bread rolls derived from Chinese women's hair? asked a female voice. No, replied a soothing light-blue voice, crusty bread rolls have been banned from using such ingredients.

When Regina opened her eyes again, the heavenly palate whose roof arched over her was already darkening. Right at the front, very far away, a pair of white fluffy teeth was hidden, the food there was real. For a moment, a nano-second, Gina felt like a little rat caught in a giant trap. But what was the point of these pangs of nostalgia, or belief in a controlling system. In the time before dot.com they might have speculated whether she was in control or being controlled, and guessed wrong every time. Gina smiled as she had a good look at her nipples in the mirror one more time before she left. The lacquer was untouched.

Summertime

Durs Grünbein

A mild evening in March, the clocks have just gone forward, it stays light for longer, remarkably light. With my window open I can hear the birds twittering, in a way I haven't heard for a long time, a clear, long drawn-out twittering reminiscent of forest clearings, in the middle of Berlin. The day draws out for a while longer, the voices of the starlings, chaffinches, tits, and blackbirds drift into these depths of space. It could be midday forty years ago, birdsong in a city swept bare by the war, over the mountains of debris, the diligent rubble trains, around the banks of a bomb crater. Or dusk a hundred years later, between the glass fronts of the high-rises in deserted downtown. Or in the year 1207, outside the gates of a town north of the Alps...do you hear me, Walther? I can hear your voice clearly within this soundscape of birds-before-sunset. And you, Jannequin? Are these not what your bird chorales are—open-air concerts of the great euthanasia-symphony, the last rites for the evening's finale? Time at a standstill and I'm all ears... Walther, come on... Tandaradei.

Notes on the Authors

1. **Siegfried Kracauer** (1889–1966). Born in Frankfurt, Kracauer became an influential critic, theorist, and writer. He left Germany for Paris and then moved to the USA in 1941, where he died in New York. This description of the modern city was originally published in the *Frankfurter Zeitung* in 1931 and collected with other urban reportage in *Straßen in Berlin und anderswo* (Streets in Berlin and Elsewhere).

2. **Alfred Döblin** (1878–1957). Döblin, born in Stettin (now Szczecin in Poland) to a Jewish family, is best known for his novel *Berlin Alexanderplatz*. In this story the narrator wanders the streets surrounding the more famous Alexanderplatz, many now renamed; it is from a posthumous collection *Die Zeitlupe* (Slow Motion).

3 & 4. **Kurt Tucholsky** (1890–1935) was born in Berlin and was one of the most prominent journalists and satirists of the Weimar Republic. He died of an overdose in Sweden in 1935, having left Germany before the rise of the National Socialists. His sketches here capture the Berliners as much as their city; a street in East Berlin is named after him.

5. **Günter Kunert** was born in Berlin in 1929 and has published very many books of poetry, prose, essays and other writing, much of which depicts Berlin. He lived in East Berlin but left for the West in 1979. This story from a 1968

collection unusually uses surreal imagery to deal with the serious historical subject of the Nazi regime and forced exile.

6. **Wolfdietrich Schnurre** (1920–1989) was born in Frankfurt am Main and moved to Berlin after the end of World War Two, initially living in East Berlin before moving to the West. This story is taken from an autobiographical 'novel in stories', *Als Vaters Bart noch rot war* (When Father's Beard was still Red) published in 1958, about a father and son.

7. **Uwe Johnson** (1934–1984), was born in Kammin (now Kamień Pomorski in Poland) and died in Sheerness on Sea where he had lived since 1974. Having studied in the GDR, Johnson moved from the East to West Berlin in 1959. This prose text is a postscript from 1970 to his well-known essay, 'Berliner S-Bahn (veraltet)', written in 1961 but rendered out of date when the Berlin Wall went up on 13 August 1961.

8. **Monika Maron**, born 1941 in Berlin, grew up in the GDR as the stepdaughter of a GDR Minister. Her first books were published only in the West and she moved to Hamburg in 1988. This autobiographical story appeared in a collection of Berlin tales, *Geburtsort Berlin* (Place of Birth: Berlin), illustrated with photos taken by her son Jonas.

9. **Julia Franck** was born in East Berlin in 1970; her family moved to West Berlin in 1978. In this story from the collection *Bauchlandung* (Belly Flop), a family flee to the refugee camp Marienfelde in West Berlin, a subject which Franck revisits in her novel *Lagerfeuer* (Camp Fire).

10. **Emine Sevgi Özdamar**, born in Malatya, Turkey in 1946, is an actress and author. She first came to Berlin as a 'guest worker' (Gastarbeiter) and worked in a factory, returning in 1976 to work with Benno Besson at the Volksbühne theatre. Her

autobiographical novel *Seltsame Sterne starren zur Erde* (Strange Stars Stare Towards Earth) rewrites some of the anecdotes first narrated in the story here.

11. **Inka Bach** was born in East Berlin in 1956 and left for West Berlin with her family in 1972. Squatting, the focus of this story, was part of the alternative scene and the radical politics in West Berlin in the 1970s and 1980s.

12. **Annett Gröschner**, born in Magdeburg in 1964, lives in Berlin. She has published a number of reportage and fictional texts set in Berlin. The story here takes inspiration from the remains of the Hotel Esplanade on Potsdamer Platz which have been preserved under glass in the Sony Centre.

13. **Carmen Francesca Banciu** was born in Lipova, Romania (1955) and came to Berlin in 1990 after the Romanian revolution. She has published in Romanian and now writes in German. The stories in *Berlin ist mein Paris* (Berlin is My Paris), from which this story is taken, were written in the Café Adler, right next to Checkpoint Charlie.

14. **Larissa Boehning** was born in Wiesbaden in 1971 and moved to Berlin in 1993. The story here is taken from her debut collection *Schwalbensommer* (Swallows' Summer) and first appeared in *Decapolis: Tales from Ten Cities* (Comma Press, 2006), edited by Maria Crossan.

15. **Fridolin Schley** was born in 1976 in Munich. This story depicts the fate of the Palace of the Republic, a GDR building condemned after the end of that state, ostensibly due to asbestos contamination; the decision to replace the Palace with the old Prussian Schloss (castle) sparked controversy in Berlin. The narrator's father is based on the chief architect of the Palace, Heinz Graffunder. While the Palace was being

demolished, it was home to a number of temporary artistic installations and events.

16. **Kathrin Röggla** was born in 1971 and grew up in Salzburg. She has lived in Neukölln in Berlin since 1996, and writes for theatre and radio as well as prose. This story from *Irres Wetter* (Strange Weather) captures Berlin's nightlife.

17. **Wladimir Kaminer** was born in Moscow in 1967 and moved to Berlin in 1990, where he runs the infamous 'Russian Disco' and broadcasts on Radio Multikulti in addition to writing. His comic texts appear in newspapers and magazines as well as numerous books, including *Ich bin kein Berliner* (I Am Not a Berliner). This short text is taken from *Russendisko* (Russian Disco), his first publication.

18. **Ulrike Draesner** was born in Munich in 1962 and writes poetry as well as prose fiction; she also translates from English. The poetic, erotic story of 'Gina Regina' was first published in the collection *Hot Dogs*.

19. **Durs Grünbein**, born in Dresden in 1962, lives in Berlin and is well known primarily as a poet. This prose poem was later revised and appeared in his diary-style *Das erste Jahr: Berliner Aufzeichnungen* (The First Year: Berlin Sketches), as the entry for 21 March 2000.

Further Reading

Guide Books

There are any number of guide books to Berlin; in addition to guides by *Rough Guide, Time Out, Lonely Planet* and *Baedeker*, Berlin's reputation for decadence and design is reflected in the editions by *Wallpaper** and *Hedonist's Guide*, and in particular guides by *Taschen* to *shops & more, restaurants & more*, amongst others.

Berlin's equivalent of *Time Out, Zitty*, also produces the *Zitty Berlin Buch* each year, with some information in English.

Jakob Hein's *Gebrauchsanweisung für Berlin* (Piper 2006) and Wladimir Kaminer's *Ich bin kein Berliner* (Goldmann 2007; also available on CD) are both comic guidebooks based on personal anecdotes.

History and Reference Books about Berlin

Faust's Metropolis, by Alexandra Richie (Harper Collins 1998). Comprehensive and detailed history of Berlin from its beginnings in the sandy soil of Brandenburg.

Berlin, by David Clay Large (Basic Books 2000). Readable history focusing on the city's culture in particular from the 19th century when Berlin became capital of a unified Germany.

The Berlin Wall, by Frederick Taylor (Bloomsbury 2006). History of the city's most (in)famous landmark.

The Ghosts of Berlin, by Brian Ladd (University of Chicago Press 1997). Accessible analysis of the historical sites in the contemporary city.

Berlin: Portrait of a City, by Hans Christian Adam (Taschen 2007). Enormous coffee table book with stunning photographs of Berlin through the years.

German Short Stories and Prose about Berlin

Summerhouse, Later, by Judith Hermann, translated by Margot Bettauer Dembo (Flamingo, Ecco 2002) and *Nothing but Ghosts*, by Judith Hermann, translated by Margot Bettauer Dembo (HarperPerennial 2005). Two collections of short stories set largely in Berlin by one of the foremost writers of a new generation.

Russian Disco, by Wladimir Kaminer, translated by Michael Hulse (Ebury Press 2002). Comic anecdotes about life in the city.

What I Saw: Reports from Berlin 1920–33, by Joseph Roth, translated by Michael Hofmann (Granta 2003). Reportage from Weimar-era Berlin, elegantly translated and introduced by poet Hofmann.

Berlin Childhood Around 1900, by Walter Benjamin, translated by Howard Eiland (Harvard University Press 2006). Distinguished theorist's recollections of turn-of-the century Berlin.

Delusions, Confusions and *The Poggenpuhl Family*, by Theodor Fontane, edited by Peter Demetz (Continuum 1997); the former also recently translated by Katharine Royce as *Trials and Tribulations* (Mondial 2009). Two charming novellas showing Berlin at the end of the 19th century, when it was only just becoming a metropolis and capital city.

German Novels about Berlin

The Wall Jumper, by Peter Schneider, translated by Leigh Hafrey (Penguin 2005). Introduced by Ian McEwan, who has himself written a couple of novels about Berlin.

Berlin Alexanderplatz, by Alfred Döblin, translated by Eugene Jolas (Continuum 1997). Döblin's classic modernist novel.

Fabian: The Story of a Moralist, by Erich Kästner, translated by Cyrus Brooks (Libris 1989). Kästner is perhaps best known for his children's book *Emil and the Detectives*, also set in Berlin; this novel presents his anti-hero Fabian in Berlin just before the rise of the National Socialists.

The Artificial Silk Girl, by Irmgard Keun, translated by Katharina von Ankum (Other Press 2002). The original 'It girl' in German literature.

Too Far Afield, by Günter Grass, translated by Krishna Winston (Faber & Faber 2001). Nobel Prize-winning author Grass's Berlin novel, influenced by Theodor Fontane.

Heroes Like Us, by Thomas Brussig, translated by John Brownjohn (Farrar Straus & Giroux 1996). Scurrilous account of the fall of the Berlin Wall, by a fantasist narrator.

Berlin Blues, by Sven Regener, translated by John Brownjohn (Secker & Warburg 2003). Regener is the lead singer of a rock band, Element of Crime; his comic novel set in West Berlin at the end of the 1980s has also been filmed as *Herr Lehmann*.

The Berlin Novels, by Christopher Isherwood (Vintage 1993).

Classic German Short Stories

There are collections of short stories in English translation by many distinguished writers, among them Franz Kafka, Heinrich Böll, Heinrich von Kleist, ETA Hoffmann, Bertolt Brecht, Thomas Mann, as well as several bilingual anthologies.

Penguin parallel texts: *German Short Stories 1*, edited by Richard Newnham and *German Short Stories 2*, edited by David Constantine.

Short Stories in German: Erzählungen auf Deutsch, edited by Ernst Zillekens (Penguin).

Deutsche Erzählungen: German Stories, translated and edited by Harry Steinhauer (University of California Press 1992). A bilingual anthology of some of the most well-known authors.

Publisher's Acknowledgements

1. Siegfried Kracauer, 'Aus dem Fenster gesehen' from *Straßen in Berlin und anderswo*. Suhrkamp 1964.

2. Alfred Döblin, 'Östlich um den Alexanderplatz' from *Die Zeitlupe*. Walter Verlag 1962.

3 & 4. Kurt Tucholsky, 'Abends nach sechs' and ''n Augenblick mal –!' from *Ausgewählte Werke*. Rowohlt 1965.

5. Günter Kunert, 'Alltägliche Geschichte einer Berliner Straße' from *Die Beerdigung findet in aller Stille statt*. Carl Hanser 1968.

6. Wolfdietrich Schnurre, 'Die Leihgabe' from *Als Vaters Bart noch rot war*. Arche 1958.

7. Uwe Johnson, 'Nachtrag zur S-Bahn' from *Berliner Sachen: Aufsätze*. Suhrkamp 1975.

8. Monika Maron, 'Geburtsort Berlin' from *Geburtsort Berlin*. Fischer 2003.

9. Julia Franck, 'Der Hausfreund' from *Bauchlandung*. DuMont 2000.

10. Emine Sevgi Özdamar, 'Mein Berlin' from *Der Hof im Spiegel*. Kiepenheuer & Witsch 2001.

11. Inka Bach, 'Besetzer' from *Bahnhof Berlin*, ed. Katja Lange-Müller. Deutscher Taschenbuchverlag 1997.

12. Annett Gröschner, 'Rest Esplanade' from *Die Stadt nach der Mauer*, ed. Jürgen Jakob Becker and Ulrich Janetzki. Ullstein 1998.

13. Carmen Francesca Banciu, 'Für eine Hand voll Kleingeld' from *Berlin ist mein Paris*. Ullstein 2002.

14. Larissa Boehning, 'Zaungäste' from *Schwalbensommer*. Eichborn 2003. Reprinted by kind permission of Comma Press.

15. Fridolin Schley, 'Das Herz der Republik' from *Wildes schönes Tier*. Berlin Verlag 2007.

16. Kathrin Röggla, 'fraktionen' from *Irres Wetter*. Residenz 2000.

17. Wladimir Kaminer, 'Stadtführer Berlin' from *Russendisko*. Goldmann 2000.

18. Ulrike Draesner, 'Gina Regina' from *Hot Dogs*. Luchterhand 2004.

19. Durs Grünbein, 'Sommerzeit' from *Bahnhof Berlin*, ed. Katja Lange-Müller. Deutscher Taschenbuchverlag 1997.

Although every effort has been made to trace and contact copyright holders prior to publication this has not been possible in every case. If notified, the publisher will be pleased to rectify any omissions at the earliest opportunity.

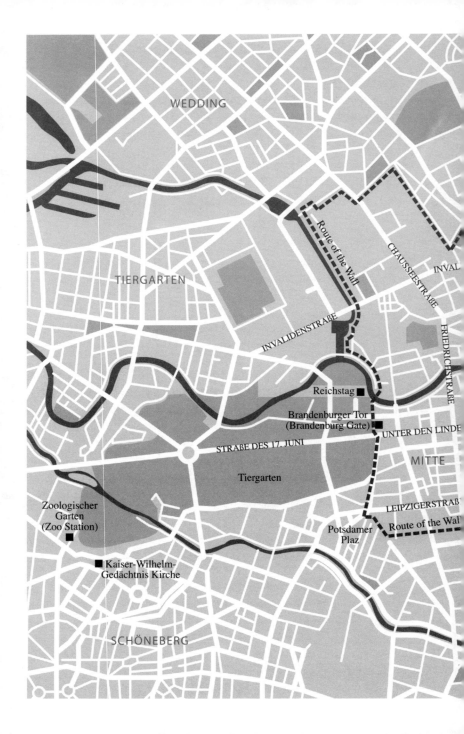

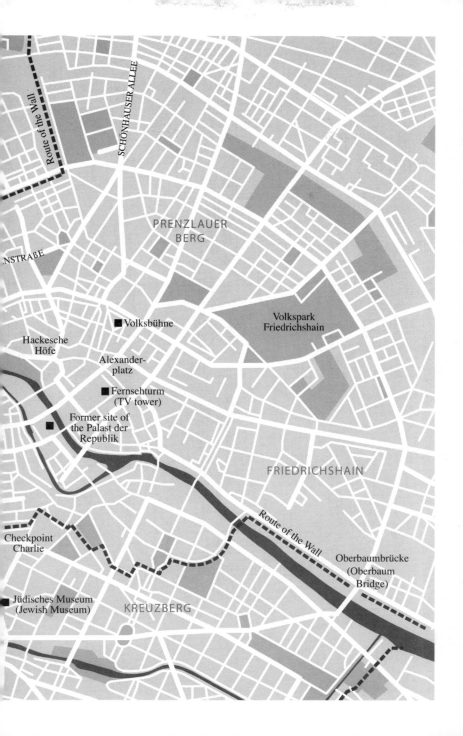

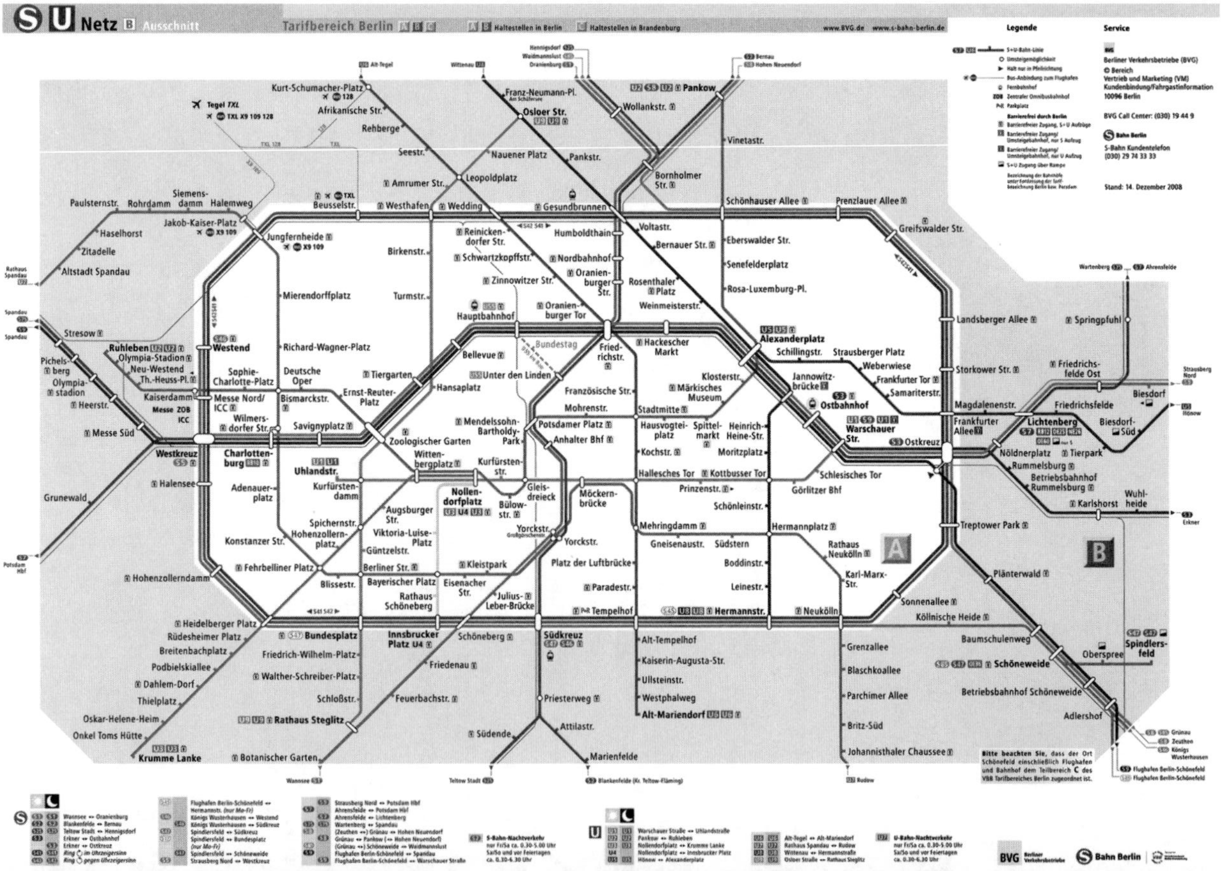

S U Netz B Ausschnitt
Tarifbereich Berlin A B C
A B Haltestellen in Berlin
C Haltestellen in Brandenburg
www.BVG.de www.s-bahn-berlin.de
Legende
Service
Berliner Verkehrsbetriebe (BVG)
© Bereich
Vertrieb und Marketing (VM)
Kundenbindung/Fahrgastinformation
10096 Berlin
BVG Call Center: (030) 19 44 9
S-Bahn Kundentelefon
(030) 29 74 33 33
Stand: 14. Dezember 2008
Tegel TXL
TXL X9 109 128
Kurt-Schumacher-Platz
Afrikanische Str.
Rehberge
Seestr.
Amrumer Str.
Leopoldplatz
Nauener Platz
Franz-Neumann-Pl.
Osloer Str.
Pankstr.
Wollankstr.
Pankow
Vinetastr.
Bornholmer Str.
Schönhauser Allee
Prenzlauer Allee
Greifswalder Str.
Gesundbrunnen
Wedding
Westhafen
Beusselstr.
Jungfernheide
X9 109
Jakob-Kaiser-Platz
Paulsternstr.
Rohrdamm
Siemensdamm
Halemweg
Haselhorst
Zitadelle
Altstadt Spandau
Rathaus Spandau
Spandau
Stresow
Pichelsberg
Olympia-Stadion
Ruhleben
Olympia-Stadion
Neu-Westend
Th.-Heuss-Pl.
Kaiserdamm
Messe ZOB ICC
Heerstr.
Messe Süd
Westkreuz
Grunewald
Halensee
Westend
Sophie-Charlotte-Platz
Messe Nord/ICC
Wilmersdorfer Str.
Charlottenburg
Mierendorffplatz
Richard-Wagner-Platz
Deutsche Oper
Bismarckstr.
Birkenstr.
Turmstr.
Reinickendorfer Str.
Schwartzkopffstr.
Zinnowitzer Str.
Hauptbahnhof
Humboldthain
Nordbahnhof
Oranienburger Str.
Oranienburger Tor
Voltastr.
Bernauer Str.
Rosenthaler Platz
Weinmeisterstr.
Eberswalder Str.
Senefelderplatz
Rosa-Luxemburg-Pl.
Alexanderplatz
Hackescher Markt
Friedrichstr.
Bundestag
Bellevue
Tiergarten
Unter den Linden
Hansaplatz
Ernst-Reuter-Platz
Savignyplatz
Zoologischer Garten
Uhlandstr.
Kurfürstendamm
Adenauerplatz
Wittenbergplatz
Mendelssohn-Bartholdy-Park
Potsdamer Platz
Anhalter Bhf
Französische Str.
Mohrenstr.
Stadtmitte
Hausvogteiplatz
Spittelmarkt
Märkisches Museum
Klosterstr.
Heinrich-Heine-Str.
Moritzplatz
Kochstr.
Hallesches Tor
Kottbusser Tor
Prinzenstr.
Schönleinstr.
Mehringdamm
Gneisenaustr.
Südstern
Hermannplatz
Boddinstr.
Leinestr.
Möckernbrücke
Gleisdreieck
Kurfürstenstr.
Nollendorfplatz
Bülowstr.
Yorckstr.
Augsburger Str.
Spichernstr.
Hohenzollernplatz
Viktoria-Luise-Platz
Güntzelstr.
Konstanzer Str.
Fehrbelliner Platz
Hohenzollerndamm
Berliner Str.
Bayerischer Platz
Blissestr.
Kleistpark
Eisenacher Str.
Rathaus Schöneberg
Julius-Leber-Brücke
Platz der Luftbrücke
Paradestr.
Tempelhof
Hermannstr.
Neukölln
Rathaus Neukölln
Karl-Marx-Str.
Schillingstr.
Strausberger Platz
Weberwiese
Frankfurter Tor
Samariterstr.
Jannowitzbrücke
Ostbahnhof
Warschauer Str.
Ostkreuz
Schlesisches Tor
Görlitzer Bhf
Landsberger Allee
Springpfuhl
Storkower Str.
Friedrichsfelde Ost
Magdalenenstr.
Frankfurter Allee
Lichtenberg
Friedrichsfelde
Biesdorf
Biesdorf-Süd
Nöldnerplatz
Tierpark
Rummelsburg
Betriebsbahnhof Rummelsburg
Karlshorst
Wuhlheide
Treptower Park
Plänterwald
Sonnenallee
Köllnische Heide
Baumschulenweg
Schöneweide
Betriebsbahnhof Schöneweide
Oberspree
Spindlersfeld
Adlershof
Heidelberger Platz
Rüdesheimer Platz
Breitenbachplatz
Podbielskiallee
Dahlem-Dorf
Thielplatz
Oskar-Helene-Heim
Onkel Toms Hütte
Krumme Lanke
Bundesplatz
Friedrich-Wilhelm-Platz
Walther-Schreiber-Platz
Schloßstr.
Rathaus Steglitz
Botanischer Garten
Innsbrucker Platz U4
Schöneberg
Friedenau
Feuerbachstr.
Südkreuz
Priesterweg
Südende
Attilastr.
Marienfelde
Alt-Tempelhof
Kaiserin-Augusta-Str.
Ullsteinstr.
Westphalweg
Alt-Mariendorf
Grenzallee
Blaschkoallee
Parchimer Allee
Britz-Süd
Johannisthaler Chaussee
Bitte beachten Sie, dass der Ort Schönefeld einschließlich Flughafen und Bahnhof dem Teilbereich C des VBB Tarifbereiches Berlin zugeordnet ist.
S-Bahn-Nachtverkehr
U-Bahn-Nachtverkehr
BVG Berliner Verkehrsbetriebe
S Bahn Berlin

Also published by Oxford University Press

PARIS TALES

Chosen and translated by Helen Constantine

Stories old and new, from each of the capital's arrondissements and quartiers

'Would-be flâneurs and Paris lovers will enjoy Helen Constantine's collection. What emerges . . . is a powerful affinity between Paris and the fantastic.' *Times Literary Supplement*

'A smartly mixed cocktail of 22 Parisian tales.' *The Independent*

'An excellent and wide-ranging collection.' *The Times*

FRENCH TALES

Chosen and translated by Helen Constantine

A story from each of France's 22 regions. 'Many of these stories are "travellers' tales", written because their authors, like Robert Louis Stevenson in the Cévennes, had good stories to tell.' *Helen Constantine*

'Immensely enjoyable.' *France Magazine*

'An intriguing collection.' *The Times*

'The tales have been translated elegantly.' *Times Literary Supplement*